"We were attack[ed]"

"We were what? I thought this was an accident." Abigail could tell by Reed's expression that he hadn't meant to reveal so much.

"I never looked at the faces of the men in the truck," she said. "Maybe if I had, I'd have gotten over my temporary amnesia and recognized them."

"Or maybe they had a beef with cops and wanted to take one out," Reed countered. "You can't be sure they intended to hurt you."

"Hurt me?" Abigail gave a cynical chuckle. "If it was connected to the attack by the beach, I suspect somebody wanted to do more than just hurt me."

She swallowed hard. "I think they hoped to permanently eliminate the threat. Namely, me."

TRUE BLUE K-9 UNIT:

These police officers fight for justice
with the help of their brave canine partners.

Valerie Hansen was thirty when she awoke to the presence of the Lord in her life and turned to Jesus. She now lives in a renovated farmhouse on the breathtakingly beautiful Ozark Plateau of Arkansas and is privileged to share her personal faith by telling the stories of her heart for Love Inspired. Life doesn't get much better than that!

Books by Valerie Hansen

Love Inspired Suspense

True Blue K-9 Unit

Trail of Danger

Emergency Responders

Fatal Threat
Marked for Revenge

Military K-9 Unit

Bound by Duty
Military K-9 Unit Christmas
"Christmas Escape"

Classified K-9 Unit

Special Agent

Rookie K-9 Unit

Search and Rescue
Rookie K-9 Unit Christmas
"Surviving Christmas"

Visit the Author Profile page at Harlequin.com for more titles.

TRAIL OF DANGER

VALERIE HANSEN

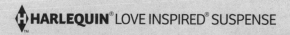

HARLEQUIN® LOVE INSPIRED® SUSPENSE

Special thanks and acknowledgment are given to Valerie Hansen for her contribution to the True Blue K-9 Unit miniseries.

Recycling programs
for this product may
not exist in your area.

LOVE INSPIRED BOOKS

ISBN-13: 978-1-335-67917-8

Trail of Danger

www.Harlequin.com

Printed in U.S.A.

Train up a child in the way he should go:
and when he is old, he will not depart from it.
–Proverbs 22:6

Special thanks to my fellow authors Lynette Eason, Dana Mentink, Laura Scott, Lenora Worth, Terri Reed, Sharon Dunn, Shirlee McCoy and Maggie K. Black, as well as to our editor, Emily Rodmell. This was a wonderful group of women chosen to portray the courage and dedication of NYC officers and K-9s.

It was a true honor.

ONE

Abigail Jones stared at the blackening eastern sky and shivered. She was more afraid of the strangers lingering in the shadows along the Coney Island boardwalk than she was of the summer storm brewing over the Atlantic. Thankfully, the air wasn't uncomfortably cool. It would be several months before she'd have to start worrying about the street kids in her outreach program during frigid New York weather.

Early September humidity made the salty oceanic atmosphere feel sticky while the wind whipped loose tendrils of Abigail's long red hair against her freckled cheeks. If sixteen-year-old Kiera Underhill hadn't insisted where and when their secret rendezvous must take place, Abigail would have stopped to speak with some of the other teens she was passing. Instead, she made a beeline for the spot where their favorite little hot dog wagon spent its days.

Besides the groups of partying youth, she

skirted dog walkers, couples strolling hand in hand and an old woman leaning on a cane. There was no sign of Kiera. That was troubling. So was the sight of a tall man and enormous dog ambling toward her. As they passed beneath an overhead vapor light, she recognized his police uniform and breathed a sigh of relief. Most K-9 patrols in her nearby neighborhood used German shepherds, so seeing the long floppy ears and droopy jowls of a bloodhound brought a smile despite her uneasiness.

Pausing, Abigail rested her back against the fence surrounding a currently closed amusement park, faced into the wind and waited for the K-9 cop to go by. His unexpected presence could be what was delaying Kiera. Street kids were wary. Once he and his dog were far enough away, the teenager would probably show herself.

"Come on, Kiera. I came alone, just like you wanted," Abigail muttered.

Actually calling out to the girl would be futile. Between the whistling wind and small groups of rowdy youth, there was no way she'd be heard. "Too bad I left my bullhorn at home," she joked, intending to relieve her own tension.

Kiera had sounded panicky when she'd phoned. That was concerning. *Ah, but she's a teenage girl*, Abigail reminded herself. *They can be real drama queens.*

"Here. Over here," drifted on the wind. Abigail strained to listen. Heard it again. "Over here."

The summons seemed to be coming from inside the Luna Park perimeter fence. That was not good since the amusement facility was currently closed. Nevertheless, she cupped her hands around her eyes and peered through the chain-link fence, trying to make out a human figure among the deep shadows. It was several seconds before she realized the gate was ajar. *Uh-oh. Bad sign.* "Kiera? Is that you?"

A disembodied voice answered faintly. "Help me! Hurry."

Abigail's heart was in her throat. If the teenager was inside the park, she was trespassing. Looking around nervously, Abigail gave the gate a slight push and it swung open on squeaky metal hinges. An icy shiver shot up her spine despite the muggy night. Something was definitely wrong. "Kiera?" Her mouth was cottony, her insides quivering. "It's Abby. I'm at the gate. You shouldn't be in there. Come on out."

As an outreach coordinator for troubled teens, Abigail was basically charged with taking care of those who came into her office. However, her past had been rough enough to compel her to respond to the girl's summons and venture out tonight. That was one of the reasons she was so successful. She was able to personally identify with the street kids she was trying to aid.

And this one sure sounded as if she was in trouble. "Kiera. Come out."

"Help me."

There it was again. A plea that Abigail could not ignore. She'd have to trespass herself in order to set the girl straight about respecting the law.

Checking to make sure the officer and his dog were far enough away to keep from spooking the girl, Abigail sidled through the gate. Although she could have enlisted his aid, she didn't want to give Kiera the mistaken notion that she had broken her promise and called the police.

Lingering odors of popcorn and other food would have been a lot more pleasant fresh. "Kiera? C'mon, honey. We shouldn't be in here. Let's go back to the boardwalk."

Pausing, Abigail listened. Thunder rumbled. Wind whistled. Paper trash that the cleaning crews had missed tumbled along the ground and began to pile up against the fences and bases of the silent rides.

Abigail couldn't help feeling edgy. She, who took pains to never break the law, was currently doing so. Yes, she had a good reason, but that didn't mean it was legal. She looked heavenward briefly and prayed, "Please, Father, show me what to do now?"

A noise to the far left startled her. She froze, straining to listen and peering into the shadows. Lightning flashed. In that instant she did see a person. Two people, to be exact. And they were men. *Imposing men.* Neither of them looked a bit like the slim young girl she was seeking.

Then, the men stepped apart and a third figure appeared between them. This person did resemble Kiera and seemed to be struggling to break away. Of all the situations Abigail had faced in her troubled past, this was the kind she'd most feared. The scenario that had given her untold nightmares.

Despite being unarmed and alone, she knew she had to do something. *What?* How could she possibly rescue Kiera, or whoever the smaller person was, without weapons? Fear urged flight. Duty insisted she act. Good sense demanded both.

How long had it been since she'd seen the police officer and his dog? Maybe she could return to the gate and call him back to rescue the captive.

But first, she had to distract the kidnappers, slow them down. Ducking behind a post, she took full advantage of the deep shadows, cupped her hands around her mouth and yelled, "Let.

Her. Go!" It worked so well she almost cheered. The men froze and stared in the direction of her voice.

As she pivoted to make a dash for the gate, lightning illuminated the area around her like the noon sun. Someone shouted, "There she is! Get her!"

Oh, no! Abigail's heart leaped. She stumbled and almost went to her knees trying to get a running start. Her pulse was pounding. Her body felt numb, as if it belonged to a stranger.

She gasped, nearly falling a second time. Shouts were getting louder, closer, more menacing.

Almost there!

A gloved hand reached past her and shoved the gate closed, blocking her exit. Someone had a death grip on the back of her lacy vest. She twisted and shed the garment. Her attacker flung it aside and grabbed her arm.

She ducked and wrenched. Pulled and flailed. It was no use.

Finally, she filled her lungs and screamed. High, loud and repeatedly. "Help!"

Officer Reed Branson's K-9 partner, Jessie, stopped plodding along with her nose to the boardwalk, lifted her broad head and looked back.

"What is it, girl?" Reed also listened. Whatever his K-9 was hearing was too faint for human ears. Nevertheless, he trusted his partner and reversed their direction. They could try to pick up Snapper's trail later, assuming the latest supposed sighting of the missing police dog was a valid lead. So far, none of the other tips had turned up the valuable and beloved German shepherd.

Jessie picked up speed, ears flopping, hips swaying beneath rolls of extra hide meant to protect her in battle.

He strained to hear despite the rushing wind and the dog's panting. His demeanor as he passed small groups of teenagers this time was different enough to scatter them. Adults cast wary glances and shied away, too.

Jessie led him straight to a gate at Luna Park. The chain was unfastened, the padlock hanging open on the wire mesh. He reached for his mic and identified himself, then said, "Ten-thirteen at entrance C, Luna Park. Possible break-in."

Dispatch answered in his earpiece. "Copy. Ten-thirteen. Requested assistance dispatched. Advise on a ten-fifty-six."

Good question. Did he need an ambulance as well as police backup? He hoped not. Hot summer nights were notorious for mischief and simmering tempers, whereas cold weather kept many New Yorkers off the boardwalk, particularly when rain was threatening. This night was a mix of both. Unpredictable.

Reed tightened his hold on Jessie's leash, pushed open the gate and undid the snap on his holster, just in case. The seasoned K-9 was on high alert, stopping to check out a small item of clothing crumpled on the ground. Reed picked it up. It was pristine, not like something that had been discarded when the park was last open. Instinct told him it was time to put Jessie to work. He presented it to her.

She was sniffing, showing eagerness to track, when a muffled noise in the distance put her hackles up and she gave voice as only a bloodhound can. Her mix of a growl, bark and then deep howl carried throughout the park, bouncing off the uneven surfaces to echo back as if a dozen hunting dogs were pursuing fleeing game.

The hardest thing for Reed, as a handler, was convincing the born and bred tracker to be silent. He laid a hand against the side of her muzzle. "Hush, Jessie. Quiet."

Slurping and drooling, she danced at his feet, mouth only temporarily closing. That was enough. Reed heard it now. A woman's scream. He grabbed the mic again as he gave Jessie her head and broke into a run. "I'm ten-eighty-nine, foot pursuit, inside Luna Park. I can hear a woman screaming."

The high-pitched protest continued, then broke off, then started again. Reed lengthened Jessie's lead but kept a firm hold of her leash so she wouldn't race into danger alone. She wasn't trained as an attack or protection dog, meaning she was nearly as vulnerable as whoever was yelling for help.

Except dogs have big teeth, he countered. Judging by the tone and volume of the screams he'd heard, this victim was not only female but likely young.

Suddenly, the night went silent. Jessie slowed, tilted her head to the side and tested the air for odors. Reed strained to listen. Nothing.

He gathered up the extra length of leash and gripped the handful tightly, every sense keen, every muscle taut. His K-9 acted puzzled for a few seconds, then started to strain to the left. Their quarry, or victim, or whatever, was apparently on the move.

Reed presented the vest again, braced himself, commanded, "Seek!" and they were off like a shot.

Abigail kicked and clawed and threw herself from side to side, trying to break loose as the first man picked her up like a sack of potatoes and jogged through the park to where the other waited. Frantic, she searched the dimness for the smaller person she'd spotted earlier. There was no sign of her or him. That was some relief. Now she could concentrate on her own escape without worrying about collateral damage to anyone else. "Let go! You're hurting me."

Her captor set her on her feet, kept hold of her wrist, and focused on his partner. "What happened to the other one?"

The second man snorted. "Almost got away. I was tyin' her to a post so I could go help you when she ran off. I caught her and locked her in the car trunk."

"As long as that took you, it's a good thing I didn't need any help." Shoving Abigail forward, he cursed.

The second man huffed wryly. "Hey, you ain't the boss."

"Neither are you."

"Never mind that. What made you think it was a good idea to bring that one back here where she could see my face?"

"Your ugly face, you mean. I had to do something with her, didn't I? She was watching us when we…"

"Shut your yap. You ain't got a brain in your pinhead."

"Oh, yeah?"

"Yeah."

Abigail felt a slight lessening of his grip. The

more the two thugs concentrated on each other, the less attention they paid to her. It took enormous effort to relax her arm and give the impression she was no longer struggling to break free.

"So, what're we gonna do?"

"How should I know?"

"What about keepin' this one? A bird in the hand?"

"Too old. See?" The captor released her arm and started to grab her shoulders, apparently intending to turn her around for his partner's inspection. Before he could get a fresh grip, Abigail continued her spin, kicked one of the men in the side of his knee and punched the other in the stomach.

Neither blow was serious but together they were enough. Abigail ducked, dodged and sprinted away. Adrenaline gave her speed and made her feel invincible. For a few seconds.

Then they were after her again. Shouting. Cursing at her and at each other. Abigail had barely enough breath to keep going. Her initial burst of speed was waning fast. Where could she hide? How close were they? She didn't dare look back.

The night became surreal. Surroundings blurred as if she were navigating a nightmare. An impressive antique carousel loomed ahead.

Despite knowing the ride was closed, she imagined seeing its wooden horses prance and paw the air. Her brain whirling, her lungs fighting to fill, she made a critical decision.

After vaulting over a low decorative fence, Abigail gained the circular platform with a leap and made a lunge for the closest steed. Her arms closed around its carved nose and she used her momentum to swing past to the second row. The horses grew uniformly smaller as she worked her way toward the center control booth. It had a door she could close. Even if it wouldn't lock, maybe her pursuers would overlook her in there.

Abigail jumped down and landed with both palms against the mirrored center pillar. Circled looking for the camouflaged door. Found it. Threw herself inside and pulled it closed behind her, stumbling backward as she did so and landing against a bank of switches.

Suddenly, calliope music began, slowly rising in speed and volume until the air vibrated. Had she bumped something? Accidentally flipped a switch? Was her hiding place useless? Undoubtedly. And it was already too late to stop the music. The damage had been done.

Stunned, she clamped her hands over her ears, pressed her back against a side wall and began a slow-motion slide to the floor as sheer panic began to dull her senses and render her helpless.

The walls pressed in on her. Reality receded as her mind shut down, and she gladly accepted the enveloping darkness of unconsciousness.

TWO

Reed and Jessie had detoured past the Shoot-the-Chutes when the calliope music had begun to play, starting low and winding up to quickly gain intensity. During the day when the park was crowded and other attractions were operating, the distinctive tunes blended in. Tonight, the solo music was deafening. And eerie, particularly since the rest of the ride wasn't lit or moving.

Jessie would have tried to climb the sides of the water ride and plunged through the cascading stream if Reed had not guided her around. The screaming had stopped. As painful as it had been to hear someone in that much distress, this was far worse. Silence could mean the danger had eased, but he knew it was more likely that things had worsened. A screeching victim was a breathing victim. It was as simple as that.

Reed approached a low fence that kept riders from cutting the line. A hand signal sent Jessie leaping over and he followed. Man-sized shadows shifted on the opposite side of the wide, round platform. Reed looked to his dog, read her body language and drew his sidearm. "Police. Freeze."

The figures froze all right—for a heartbeat—then parted and dashed off in opposite directions. Not only could Reed not pursue them both, he still didn't know where the screaming victim was or how badly she may have been injured. Finding out came first.

"Seek!"

Jessie led him in a weaving pattern between horses while Reed radioed his position and circumstances. The K-9 went twice around the center pole of the carousel before stopping and putting her enormous paws up on one of the beveled mirrors.

"Sit. Stay," Reed commanded. The door release was cleverly hidden but he found it. "Police," he announced, his gun at the ready.

The hair on the back of his neck rose and perspiration trickled down his temples. He pulled open the narrow door and struck a marksman's pose with his gun and flashlight.

Instead of the panicking, wild-eyed victim he'd expected, he saw a small figure curled up on the cement floor. His light panned over her.

She had long, reddish hair that made him think she was a teen until he took a closer look.

He'd seen that face. Tonight. She'd passed him on the boardwalk not more than a few minutes ago. She was no kid but she wasn't middle-aged either. Reed guessed her to be younger than he was by five or ten years, which would put her in her twenties. What in the world was she doing out here in the middle of the night in the first place?

Holstering his gun, he bent and lightly touched her arm. Her skin was clammy. "Ma'am? Are you hurt?"

There was no reaction. The woman didn't even act startled when he held her wrist to take her pulse but he did notice that the fair skin looked irritated. "Can you tell me what happened?"

Still nothing. He could hardly hear himself speak over the rollicking pipe organ music. A quick scan of the control panel showed one switch out of place, so he flipped it to kill the noise. Propping the narrow door open for ventilation he stood with one booted foot outside and radioed in the details as he knew them. "That's right. She's really out of it. I don't see any serious signs of physical trauma but I can't get a response, so you'd better start medics. The victim may have internal injuries or be drugged. I'm pretty sure she was the one doing all the screaming."

He paused and listened to the dispatcher, then stated his case. "Jessie acts like this is the same person she was tracking before, and I have no reason to doubt my K-9. Put a rush on that ambulance? I don't want my victim to code while I wait, okay? I'm going to take a chance and move her out onto the carousel floor where she can get more air. Tell backup to hurry."

One more check of his surroundings and a long look at his dog assured Reed the area was clear. He bent and gently lifted the victim in his arms. She was lighter than he'd imagined. "Take it easy," he said, speaking as if to a frightened child. "I'm a police officer. You're safe now."

She stirred. Her lashes quivered.

Reed placed her carefully on one of the chariot bench seats. It was too short for her to lie down all the way so he propped up her feet and lowered her shoulders, bringing more circulation, more oxygen to her brain.

She blinked and stared directly at him. He had expected at least a tinge of leftover panic but there was none. The woman didn't even flinch as she studied him.

He gave her a minute to process her thoughts, then asked, "What happened to you? Why were you screaming?"

"Screaming? I don't think…" She coughed. "My throat hurts."

"I'm not surprised," Reed told her. "What's your name?"

The blue eyes widened and filled with tears. "It's—it's Abigail. I think."

Abigail's instincts told her to trust this man even before she realized he was wearing an NYPD uniform. He had kind brown eyes and his expression showed concern. What struck her as odd was her sense of overall peace and security in his presence.

Looking past him, she saw elaborately carved wooden carousel horses that reminded her of the ones on the restored antique ride at Luna Park. *Luna Park?* What she was doing there? And why was a police officer acting as if he thought she needed help?

"Abigail?" he asked softly. "That is your name, right?"

"Of course it is." Affirmation came easily.

"How about a last name?"

"Um… Jones?"

His lopsided smile made his eyes twinkle. It was clear he didn't believe her. Thoughts solidified in her muddled mind and affirmed her choice. "It really is Jones. I'm sure it is."

"Okay. How are you feeling? Are you hurt?"

Abigail worked her shoulders and rubbed her right arm. "I think I pulled a muscle." Her eyes widened. "Did you see something happening to me?"

Reed shook his head. "Sorry. No. By the time I got here you had stopped screaming and were hiding. All I saw were shadows."

He paused, studying her so intensely that it made her ask, "Shadows? Of who? What?"

"Don't you remember?"

Her earlier peace was giving way to the uneasiness of the unknown. How much did she remember? And why did she feel a creeping fear when she tried to draw those memories out?

Head throbbing, she sniffled and pressed her fingertips to her temples. "I don't know anything." She concentrated on her rescuer. "Why can't I remember?"

"Trauma can do that sometimes. It'll all come back to you after a bit." His radio crackled and he replied. "Copy. Tell them to pull as close as they can to the carousel. She's conscious but disoriented."

Abigail grasped his forearm. "What's wrong with me?"

"The ambulance is on scene. Medics will look you over and take good care of you from here on."

He leaned away and started to stand but she

held fast. "Don't leave me. Please? I don't even know who you are."

"Officer Reed Branson." He reached into his pocket and handed her a business card. "Hang on to this. It'll help you remember me later. I'm part of the NYC K-9 Command Unit, not a detective, so I won't be investigating your case, but you may have questions for me once you get your memory back."

"Canine?" She peered past him. "Where's your dog?"

A hand signal brought a panting, pleased-looking bloodhound to his side, where it sat obediently, staring up at him as if he were the most important person in the world. That tongue, those floppy ears, the drooling lips. Abigail almost gasped. "I remember him. I saw him somewhere."

"Out here. Tonight," Reed said. "We passed you on the boardwalk. And it's *she*. Jessie is a female."

"She found me?"

"Yes. She heard your calls for help before I did. That led us into the park, where we found this." He pulled a crumpled crocheted vest out of his pocket. "Is it yours?"

"Yes!" Abigail was thrilled to recognize it.

"Jessie used it to follow your scent. I'm a little

surprised she was able to do it so well with this storm brewing. Wind can throw trackers off."

Abigail's headache was intensifying to the point where it was upsetting her stomach. She knew she wouldn't have ventured out at night, alone, without a valid reason, so what was she supposed to be doing?

She tried to stand. The carousel and objects beyond began to move. At least, she thought they did. Given her undeniable unsteadiness, she wasn't sure if the platform beneath was spinning or if her head was. Or both.

Instinct urged her to reach out to the police officer, to draw on his strength. Instead, she covered her eyes with her hands. "I'm sorry. I get terrible headaches when a storm is coming but I've never had one this bad before."

Someone—was it her rescuer?—cupped her shoulders and guided her to the edge of the circular platform where other gentle hands lifted her down and placed her on a gurney. She could smell the bleach on the sheets. A bright beam of light stabbed into her eyes.

Abigail tried to cover her face again but someone was restraining her. A wide strap crossed her upper torso and tightened. She began to struggle. Being held so still was frightening, although she couldn't pinpoint a reason for her rising panic.

"No! Let me go!"

A low masculine voice cut through her protests and brought calm. Large hands gently touched her shoulder. "Easy, Abigail. It's okay. They're just trying to help you."

"Don't let them strap me down! Please!"

"All right." She saw Reed casually wave the medics away. "I'll be right here. Nobody will have to restrain you as long as you lie still. Understand?"

"Uh-huh."

"Good. Now let them take your blood pressure and pulse, okay?"

A strong urge to resist any involuntary movement of her arms arose as soon as one of the medics began to work on her again. Thankfully, this tech was a woman who made short work of checking her vitals, listening to her ragged breathing with a stethoscope and reporting to a doctor via radio.

The numbers quoted didn't matter to Abigail. All she cared about was having the police officer close by. It didn't occur to her that he wouldn't be able to climb into the ambulance with her until he stepped back at its door.

She reached out. "Aren't you coming?"

"Can't." The attendants paused while he explained. "I have a responsibility to Jessie, not to mention my reason for being out here tonight.

I was in the middle of a different search until you screamed."

No matter how logical his answer was, she couldn't accept it. "Promise you'll follow me? You're the only one who has any idea what happened out here."

"You'll be fine once you're under a doctor's care." The way he patted the back of her hand as he spoke reminded her of a parent trying to soothe a child who was throwing a tantrum. That unfortunate comparison was hard to take, particularly since her head was still pounding and her vision blurred whenever she moved.

Abigail jerked her hand away, turned her head and closed her eyes. "Fine. Go. Save the rest of the world if that's what you want." Tremors wracked her body. Nobody had to tell her she wasn't herself. Her conscience was doing a good job of that without any outside help. Harsh words and snappy retorts were not her usual reactions to difficulties, nor was she sarcastic. People at work were always complimenting her on her even temperament.

Work? Yes, work! She was an outreach coordinator for AFS, A Fresh Start, and helped homeless and troubled teens. That she remembered well. She could picture the tiny office in Brighton Beach, her desk stacked with file folders, and even the potted violet plant atop the book-case beneath the window.

"That's better," she whispered with a sigh, not expecting anyone to take notice.

The female medic smiled. "Good to hear." She held out a clear plastic mask fitted with a narrow tube. "Just let me give you a few breaths of oxygen and you'll feel even better."

The plastic contraption hovered over Abigail's face. There was a continuing urge to resist being treated, but now that she'd recalled more about her life, she'd settled down enough to control herself. "Okay."

Elastic straps held the mask in place. She took several deep breaths.

"That's it. Nice and slow." The medic was hovering over her, looking directly into her eyes. "Now, the law says I have to secure you before we can hit the road, so here come the straps again. I'm sorry to have to do it but I could lose my license if I didn't make sure you were safe."

Abigail inhaled more of the enriched air, then lifted the mask to speak. "I'll try to behave. I promise. I don't know what came over me before."

"Leftover trauma, if I had to guess," the woman replied pleasantly. "I almost wouldn't mind trading places with you if I could get Reed

Branson to look at me the way he looked at you just now."

"That cop?"

"Oh, yeah." She chuckled as she tightened the safety strap. "What a hunk."

"I didn't notice."

"Really?" The medic fitted her with an automatic blood pressure cuff and checked the flow of oxygen to the mask, then smiled. "Maybe you need your vision checked, too."

Reed's first duty was to notify acting chief Noah Jameson that he had diverted from his tracking assignment in order to intervene in a crime. Then he checked in with fellow police officers while they were still on scene. Some had dispersed to search the shadowy amusement park while others guarded the carousel and busy crime scene techs. The Coney Island boardwalk was relatively safe most of the time but it did draw a rougher element late at night, particularly in warm weather. A hot summer or fall day brought out every troublemaker in the state of New York at night. Or so it seemed.

Adding to the foreboding atmosphere, wind-driven rain began pelting the rides and the ground as if bent on settling a score with humanity. Reed kept Jessie fairly dry under the canopy of the carousel while CSIs dusted the control booth mirrors for fingerprints and filled tiny plastic envelopes with dust and debris from the floor of the wooden turntable.

"Needle in a haystack?" Reed asked a familiar crime scene investigator.

"More like a needle in a stack of other needles. There's virtually no chance we'll scoop up usable clues. They've probably blown all the way to Flatbush by now."

Reed nodded. "Agreed. Sorry I didn't get a better look at the guys who tried to grab the victim."

"Any chance this is connected to the rash of disappearing teens?" the CSI asked, pausing to glance up at him.

"Remotely. This victim looked pretty young until I got up close. You'd think anybody who was after kids would be able to tell the difference, though." He scowled. "I'm sorry she had to go through this, but she probably stood a better chance than an inexperienced kid would have."

"Do you know her?"

"Not the way I know you and most of these others." Reed indicated a group of NYPD regular officers sweeping the area with flashlights and sloshing through puddles. "Going by what she told me after Jessie tracked her down, her name is Abigail Jones. That's so common I didn't believe her last name until the medics found ID on her."

"Jones? I wouldn't have bought that, either."

"Are you about done here?"

"Why? You got a hot date?"

Smiling slightly, Reed denied it. "Nope. Just wondered. Chief Jameson released me and I thought I'd check on the victim before my shift ends."

The man chuckled. "Your car is going to smell like wet dog, Branson."

"Probably. It often does."

Reed had a standard-issue yellow slicker and a modified cover for Jessie, too. In his Tahoe SUV. Three blocks away. He sighed, waved goodbye to the friendly tech and stepped off the carousel.

Big drops were still falling so close together it was impossible to stay dry. Jessie snapped at a few of them as if it were a game. "You're thirsty, aren't you girl? Hang in there. I'll pour you a drink as soon as we get back to the car."

Because he was paying close attention to his dog, Reed noticed a slight change in her behavior as they walked up the street. That was part of being a K-9 handler. He and the dog were supposed to read each other without fail. And right now Jessie was acting as if she sniffed something familiar. Since Abigail was long gone, Reed could only surmise she was getting a whiff of the thugs.

He delayed radioing his suspicion until he had walked a little farther, following his dog until she paused at a curb and turned in circles several times. When she looked up at him he could tell she was disappointed.

"Well, you tried, girl," Reed said. "And I forgot to reward you the last time, didn't I?" Handing the K-9 her favorite toy, a piece of frayed mooring rope, he ducked into a doorway to call dispatch. "This is Branson, K-9 Unit. Jessie just led me to an empty parking space. It's in front of a falafel stand on West Fifteenth almost to Surf Avenue. There's a tourist trap with souvenirs next to it. We may see something on surveillance cameras if we pull up tonight's recordings."

"Copy. I'm showing you on West Fifteenth Street a little north of Bowery."

"That's affirmative. I'm about to head for the hospital to check on the victim, then I'll be ten-sixty-one. It's been a long night."

"Copy that."

Visions of Abigail's pale blue eyes and ginger hair remained vivid, not that he was pleased to have noticed. His life was complete. He had the perfect job, a peaceful private life and the best tracking dog in the unit, maybe in the whole state. The K-9s and his fellow officers, which included his sister, Lani, as a rookie, were all the *family* he needed. Theirs was a dangerous profession. Just look at what had happened to his former boss, Chief Jordan Jameson, six months ago.

The entire NYC K-9 Command Unit was still mourning deeply, as were others. Losing Jameson had been hard to accept, especially for Zack, Carter and Noah Jameson, Jordy's brothers. The glue of respect and friendship that had held their unit together had been sorely tried after Jameson's murder and Noah's interim promotion into his vacated position.

The killer had been clever, even leaving a suicide note, but Jordy's team of officers hadn't bought it. Between the four branches of the K-9 Unit—Transit, Emergency Services, Bomb Squad and Narcotics—they had all the expertise they needed to pursue the truth. To help homicide solve the crime, one way or the other. No one in his unit was content to sit back and wait for results from other divisions.

Yet life went on. It was true that New York City never slept. Reed knew what his duty was and did it to the best of his ability. Now and then, however, a puzzle came along that fascinated him enough to seek answers on his own time, such as, what had happened to Abigail Jones tonight.

THREE

"I just want to go home," Abigail kept telling anyone who entered her hospital room. What was wrong with these people? Why were her wishes being ignored?

The graying patient in the other bed snorted as a harried nurse beat a hasty retreat. "Might as well save your breath, sweetie. You ain't get-tin' out of here tonight."

Desperate for someone who would listen, Abigail fought tears of frustration as she said, "I don't understand why they won't discharge me. They did a brain scan and the doctor told me there was no damage."

"I believe he said, 'No visible damage.'"

"Same thing."

"Not hardly." The other woman coughed. "I heard him asking questions. You didn't have a lot of answers." Another cough. "You hidin' from an abusive man or avoidin' the cops?"

"Of course not!" *I'm not my mother.*

"Okay, okay, don't get your jammies in a twist. I was just askin'. What happened to you, anyway?"

Abigail chewed on her lower lip before admitting, "I don't know. I remember getting ready to leave the office. The next thing I knew it was dark and I was looking up at a stranger."

"Did he hurt you? If he did, you gotta report it, you know. We can't clean up these streets if we don't all do our part."

"I know," Abigail said sadly. "I work with homeless teens all the time."

"So what really happened to you? You can tell me. I won't breathe a word."

Frustration took over. Her voice rose, then cracked. "I don't know! I can't remember."

As she took a shaky breath there was a knock at the open door and a man in a dark blue uniform entered the room. No, not *a* man, *the* man. She might not recall anything else from her ordeal but she'd never forget Reed Branson. Or his dog.

He smiled, dark eyes twinkling. "Good to see you awake and recovering."

"Yeah. I'm pretty happy about that, too." Abigail mirrored his expression. "They tell me there's no brain damage but they won't let me go home."

Approaching her bed, he pulled up a chair and sat. "Do you know where you live?"

"Of course I do. I have an apartment in Brighton Beach."

He held up his hands, palms out. "Okay, okay. Just asking. What else have you managed to remember since I found you?"

"Not a lot." Abigail sobered. "I was just telling my new friend here that it's a blank."

"I heard part of that before I came in."

"You were eavesdropping?"

"Not exactly. You'd be surprised how often we overhear a lot more than people are willing to disclose officially. I'm not the enemy, Ms. Jones. We really are sworn to protect and serve."

Sighing, she nodded at him. "Well, at least you know I'm not holding back. I'd give almost anything to remember what made me walk over to Concy Island at night. I'm usually more cautious. Any big city like ours will rise up and bite you if you're not careful, I don't care whether you're a native or not." Studying his face, she noticed a small scar on his chin and wondered if he'd gotten that in the line of duty. Rather than spoil his looks it gave him a rugged edge.

"Will you be all right when you do go home? I mean, do you live in a secure building?"

"Why?" She inhaled sharply when she fully

grasped his implication. "You don't think anybody will come after me there, do you?"

"Probably not. I wish I knew more about the guys who were manhandling you tonight, though."

"So do I." Mulling over her predicament, she added, "I can only hope I'll recognize them soon enough to protect myself if I see them again."

"Tell you what," Reed said. "I'll go look your place over on my own time if the department doesn't send another officer to do it. How's that sound?"

Abigail frowned at him. "Why are you being so nice to me? You don't even know me."

"I'm not real sure," he admitted with a grin. "Maybe because my being in the right place at exactly the right time to rescue you seems like such an odd coincidence. Plus, I had Jessie with me. She did all the tracking. I just followed her lead. That strikes me as providential, if you get my drift."

"Why did you say were you down on the boardwalk?"

"Jessie and I were sent to follow up a tip on a missing K-9 that means a lot to the department, to my unit. Snapper is a highly trained German shepherd who used to be the chief's partner."

The flash of grief she saw pass over Reed's face took Abigail by surprise. She could understand missing a dog as if you'd lost a friend, but the officer's emotions seemed stronger than that. She had to ask. "What happened?"

When Reed swallowed hard and said, "Chief Jordan Jameson was murdered by a person or persons unknown. Snapper was his K-9 and has been missing since," her stomach knotted. He wasn't merely looking for a lost dog, he was searching for a cop killer. That made all her troubles pale in comparison.

"I'm so sorry."

"Thanks. Me, too."

Before Abigail could decide what to say next, the handsome K-9 officer got to his feet. "You take care. I'll get your address off your file, then speak to your super and make sure your apartment is safe before you're discharged. I promise."

He wheeled and was gone before she had time to decide to stop him. Pride urged her to object to having her privacy violated but good sense intervened. There was nothing secret in her life, nothing that anyone could hold against her.

Except my childhood, she added. Those records had been expunged but she hadn't hidden her past when she'd applied for the job at A Fresh Start. If anybody could understand street kids, it was her. Success proved it.

The image of a pretty blonde teen popped

into her mind. Kiera Underhill was one of her toughest cases, a girl with a chip on her shoulder the size of Lady Liberty's torch.

Abigail shivered despite the warm room. Thoughts of Kiera were unduly disturbing for some reason. A sense of foreboding had settled over her like winter fog, yet the harder she tried to access her locked mind, the more blank it became.

She scooted down in the bed and pulled a sheet over her head, blotting out the world the way she had as a little girl.

Irony brought unshed tears. If she was going to forget something traumatic and painful, why couldn't it be her childhood?

It had been several days since Reed had visited Abigail in the hospital. Why was he having so much trouble getting the pretty redhead out of his thoughts? They had no actual connection other than their accidental meeting at Luna Park, unless you counted the city's problem with homeless kids and Abigail's job assisting them. He'd had more than one difficult encounter with young teens along the boardwalk and in nearby neighborhoods like hers. Many were victims who put on a show of being capable and happy while hiding their true situation. They found safety in numbers, yes, but get one of them alone and you could often glimpse the fear lurking behind a facade of bravado and arrogance.

When he tried to phone Abigail at home and got no answer, he left messages, which she apparently ignored. Checking with her place of employment didn't help either. She'd been put on medical leave.

Consequently, he decided to visit in person, parked as close as he could, about three blocks west, and walked over with Jessie. Reed let her sniff along the narrow sidewalk because she wasn't on duty. Street-side trees that had once enhanced the old neighborhood crowded the four-and five-story brick apartment buildings as if in a battle for dominance. Eddies of sand and trash waited against the curbs for city trucks to sweep away.

After reaching Abigail's building, he found her name on the tenant list and pushed the worn brass intercom button. "Ms. Jones? It's Reed Branson." There was no answer, no buzz to unlock the front door. He tried again, speaking more slowly and identifying himself as a K-9 officer. The result was the same.

Not good. Even off-duty he needed to watch his professional image, so he hesitated before randomly pushing other buttons. A tenant leaving solved his problem. Reed grabbed the edge of the exterior door before it could close behind the other man, nodded pleasantly and slipped inside with Jessie.

Reed chose to take the stairs to the third floor rather than chance riding an elevator that was probably older than his grandfather. The halls were swept clean, which was a plus, but the ancient building exuded an aura of age and use. Cooking odors seeped into the hallways, reminding him of the street fairs he'd attended around the city.

His knock on Abigail's door was not demanding—until he got no response.

He called to her. "Ms. Jones? Abigail? It's Reed Branson. And Jessie. Are you all right?"

Still no answer. He knocked again. Louder. Called out to her, "Abigail?"

Frustration made him want to force his way in but what if she simply wasn't home? A quick trip back downstairs and he was knocking at the superintendent's door.

An apartment dweller across the hall stuck her graying head out of her own apartment and gave him a scathing look. "Hush. You're spoiling my show. I was about to find out if Reginald really murdered his half brother."

It took Reed the space of several heartbeats to realize she was referring to the plot of a daytime soap opera. "Sorry. But I can't get the tenant in 312 to come to the door and I'm worried. Do you know if she's gone out?"

"Not likely. She would have said. Does she know you?"

"Yes." Since he was in civilian clothes he flashed his badge wallet. "Officer Reed Branson. I was the one who helped her when she ran into trouble a couple of nights ago."

"Well, in that case, thank you." She stepped out. "I'm Olga Petrovski." A ring of keys jingled in her hand as she locked her door behind her. "That poor girl's a basket case and nobody seems to care. She's turning into a worse hermit than she was before. Doesn't even have a cat for company. Can you imagine?" The woman led the way up the stairs, surprising Reed with her ease of movement in broken-down shoes that looked as if they were about to fall off.

"You have keys? I thought Mr. Rosenbaum was the super."

"He is. But he's in Jersey visiting his daughter. When he's gone, I handle the building." She squinted at Jessie. "That dog better be housetrained."

Reed paced her. "She is. Jessie's a police officer, too, K-9 unit. We're just not in uniform today."

They reached Abigail's door. The woman knocked gently. "Abby, honey. It's Olga. You need to open up so we can check on you. Please?" Casting a worried look at Reed, she spoke aside. "Like I said, I look after her and she never goes out these days. She has to be in there. You didn't scare her, did you?"

He shrugged. "Not purposely. She seemed to be doing pretty well when I saw her in the hospital right after the incident but she's not returning my calls." Glancing at the woman's fisted hand he said, "I think you should use your key."

She did. The door swung open slowly. "We're coming in, dear. It's Olga and…"

"Officer Reed Branson," he called. "I brought K-9 Jessie, too. I'm sorry to disturb you."

Still there was no reply, no sign of the apartment's occupant. Heavy drapes were pulled, shutting out most of the available daylight. The odor of pizza or something equally spicy lingered, although he couldn't spot takeout containers. Abigail Jones's home was spotless yet unwelcoming. She had created her own dungeon and locked herself away in it.

Reed unclipped Jessie's leash and quietly ordered, "Seek."

Seeming to sense the need for finesse, Jessie didn't give voice to her quest. She merely snuffled along the carpet, clearly on the trail of something or someone. Reed came next, followed by the acting super.

The K-9 entered a bedroom and circled the bed, then barked once at a closet door. Reed moved in. "Abigail? Ms. Jones? It's the police. Your friend Olga from downstairs is here, too. She let us in."

He eased open the door.

Abigail pulled her knees closer. Instinct warred with the part of her mind that knew there was no real danger. She wanted to stand up and act more normal, but some inner power refused to let her move.

A clicking pattern on the bare floor jarred her. She heard heavy breathing and her heart stopped for a moment before she realized the noise was a dog's panting. A broad wet nose poked through a crack in the door. *The bloodhound!*

Jessie panted against Abigail's cheek, then slurped her ear with a tongue wide enough to cover it. That was enough stimulus to snap her out of her fugue.

She focused first on the affectionate hound and rubbed her droopy, velvety ears, then forced herself to look up at Reed and Olga. "Hi."

"Hello," Reed said.

Olga followed with, "Are you all right, hon?"

The ridiculousness of her location triggered Abigail's wry wit despite feelings of unease and embarrassment. "Fine and dandy. I always sit on the floor of my closet. Doesn't everybody?" When Reed offered his hand, she took it and let him pull her to her feet. "In other words, no."

"I get that," he said. "How about coming out here with us? I'd like to have a talk."

Abigail managed to overcome lingering reluctance by keeping one hand atop the dog's broad head. "I'm sorry I caused worry. It's just… I don't know. For some reason I couldn't make myself come to the door when you buzzed and then knocked."

"How about my phone calls? I left messages. Did you get those?"

"I—I must have. I probably didn't recognize your number and I didn't listen to anybody who had a deep voice."

"I'll go make some coffee," Olga offered. "You two have a seat and visit."

Abby chose the sofa, relieved as the police officer took an easy chair. Even in jeans and a polo shirt instead of his uniform, he had the bearing of someone in command. Someone to trust and lean on in times of trouble. Beyond the fact that she found him handsome, there was an unexplainable attraction. That, she attributed to his heroic actions. Why wouldn't she admire somebody who had rescued her the way this K-9 cop had?

To her delight, Jessie jumped onto the couch

and plopped her enormous head in Abigail's lap. It was a relief to rhythmically stroke the tan fur. "I think she likes me."

"No doubt. Are you feeling better now?"

"Yes. Thanks. I don't know what came over me."

Reed sobered. "Have you seen a doctor since you left the hospital? It's normal to be uptight after a traumatic event, but it's troubling to see you so fearful. I think you should seek professional help."

Her hand stilled. "You think I'm crazy?"

"No, no." Reed leaned forward, elbows resting on his thighs, hands clasped between his knees. "What I'm trying to say is that sometimes we need to talk it all out, to try to make sense of whatever has happened to us. Posttraumatic stress can hit anybody. Surely you've seen it in some of the homeless kids you work with."

She nodded.

"Then you know it's not a sign of weakness, Ms. Jones, it's a manifestation of your mind's self-defense mechanism. We all get scared sometimes. It's when we get stuck in that emotional state that it becomes a problem."

Abigail's fingers slipped under Jessie's collar and she wiggled them. Pure bliss filled the dog's soulful brown eyes and she actually sighed in contentment. Searching for a smidgen of similar peace, Abigail asked, "So why don't I remember my attackers?"

"Short-term amnesia, I assume. A health care professional can tell you more."

"No way. I can't afford to be judged mentally unstable. It might cost me my job. I won't abandon those kids. It's bad enough that I've stayed home as long as I have."

"Surely no one holds that against you."

Abigail huffed. "I do. I haven't been able to push myself to set foot out of this apartment all weekend."

"The trip home from the hospital went all right?"

"Yes, but I thought…"

He leaned closer. "What? You thought what?"

"You're going to think I really have lost my mind. I thought I heard the voice of one of my attackers on my way home in a taxi."

"The driver?"

"No, no. Passing on the sidewalk. A man yelled and he sounded so menacing I almost jumped out and ran."

"Where was this? What street?"

"I'm not sure. I covered my eyes."

"I can take you over the same basic route, if you want. Maybe he lives or works around there."

She was so astounded by his suggestion, she

was temporarily speechless. Finding her voice, she finally said, "Do you think I *want* to find him? No way. If I never run into him again it will be too soon."

Even as she was speaking, Abigail somehow knew a repeat encounter was possible. It didn't matter how big the city was or how carefully she moved through it, she could meet her attacker again. And until her memory recovered, she was a sitting duck for any evil he had planned. If only she could remember more. Put faces and descriptions together and help the police.

But those memories were all gone, sunken into an abyss of her own making and leaving her a prisoner in a cell with invisible bars.

FOUR

Watching Abigail unwind while petting Jessie gave Reed an idea. If she continued to refuse to see a doctor about her mental hiccup, perhaps he could help her another way.

"Jessie sure took to you. You must be a dog lover, too."

He noted a flush of her cheeks. "I don't really know. I mean, I've fed strays before but I've never had a pet of my own."

"Not even when you were a kid?"

The warmth he'd sensed was swept away by a scowl and a shake of her head. "Sometimes I wonder if I was ever a child."

Concerned, he regarded her soberly. "You're serious."

"Very."

"Care to explain?"

"Not really."

Although Abigail rested her hand atop Jessie's head, Reed noticed that she had ceased stroking. The friendly bloodhound did her best to encourage further attention, finally rolling onto her back, all four paws in the air, tail thumping the sofa cushions.

Reed waited for Jessie's antics to relax Abigail again before he mentioned his idea. "Since you're so naturally good with dogs, how about volunteering to foster one of our extra pups."

She scowled at him. "Do *what*?"

"We received an amazing working dog as a gift from the Czech Republic. Unfortunately, there must have been a miscommunication because Stella delivered a litter soon after she arrived."

"What does that have to do with me?" Abigail looked so astonished he decided to play up the underdog, literally.

"After her pups were weaned and tested for various abilities, most of them qualified for our training program and are being fostered." Reed paused for effect. "One little female is right on the cusp of flunking out and we'd like to find her a new foster home to see if lots more one-on-one attention helps. I'm not asking you to commit to giving her a permanent home but it will help her develop to her full potential if she's well socialized and loved while she's young."

Abigail was shaking her head. "I have enough problems without adding a puppy."

"You wouldn't have to keep her. Just get her off to a good start."

"Me? I can hardly handle my own life these days and you want to add an impressionable youngster to it?"

Shrugging, Reed blew out a breath that was so evident it even caught Jessie's attention. "I just figured, since you were so good at rescuing needy kids, you might be willing to do the same for an innocent animal."

Judging by the way Abigail was looking at him, Reed could tell she wasn't totally buying his analogy. "It's true. All of it," he insisted. He pulled out his phone and paged through the photo files, smiling and holding it out for her to view once he located the shot he wanted. "This is Midnight. Look at those sad eyes. How can you refuse to help her?"

The instant Abigail saw the picture, her whole body reacted and she pouted. "Oh, poor thing. She looks so lonely all by herself."

Reed let her take his phone so she could study Midnight in detail. She may have told him no but her body language said otherwise. All he had to do was be patient.

"What a sweet face. And those floppy ears. Will they stand up like a German shepherd's when she's older?"

"No. We did genetic testing on the litter.

They're purebred Labs like their mama. The only difference is, Stella's coat is yellow. That's going to be another problem in placing Midnight if she doesn't make it through our program. Black dogs are statistically the last to be chosen at the pound."

"You're not sending this poor baby to the dog pound!"

"Well, I hope not, but…"

It was all Reed could do to keep from grinning. When her eyes met his he could tell she realized he'd been leading her on.

Abigail began to smile and slowly shook her head. "You're good. I could use somebody with a smooth technique like yours at work. You could charm those wild kids into shape in no time."

His grin escaped with a quiet chuckle. "Does this mean you'll take the pup?"

"No." She handed his phone back to him. "But I will agree to meet her, no guarantees. You could fill a book with all the things I *don't* know about raising a dog."

"That's okay. I'll teach you." He stood before she could change her mind and called out to Olga. "I'll take a rain check on the coffee, ma'am."

"You're leaving?" the older woman asked, peeking around the corner from the kitchen.

"Not for long. I'll be back ASAP. I promise."

Already thinking ahead, Reed signaled to Jessie, clipped her leash to her collar and headed for the door with a brief wave goodbye. His intention was to leave before Abigail thought it through and had time to change her mind. Once she met Midnight he was pretty sure she'd fall in love.

With the dog, he added to himself when a stray thought intruded to remind him how attractive the young woman was.

Reed shook off any whispers of impropriety. He had not come there looking for romance. He'd sought out Abigail because of a sense of duty. When he'd rescued her he'd stepped into her life enough to care, which was not necessarily a wise reaction. Nevertheless, he was determined to do what he could to help. This was a win-win situation. A needy pup would help Abigail heal as well as benefit the less than stellar young dog.

He jogged down the stairs with Jessie at his side. Midnight might still blossom in the right foster home even though she'd done poorly so far. As long as he stuck around long enough to get Abigail and the pup off to a good start there was a chance of redemption. He could already see her taking Midnight to work with her when she was ready to go back. A loving puppy would help reach the street kids, too, and perhaps show aptitude as a future service dog. They needed the nonjudgmental acceptance K-9s provided.

Together, Reed and Jessie broke out into the sunshine and headed for his SUV. There was a spring in the dog's gait and she almost looked as if she was smiling.

Reed empathized. He was pretty happy, too. If the narrow sidewalk hadn't been so crowded he might have jogged back to his vehicle instead of settling for a brisk walking pace.

Suddenly, Jessie gave a tug on the leash that jarred Reed out of his reverie. He paused. Looked behind him. Heard the bloodhound growl and saw the hackles on her back bristle.

"What is it, girl?"

Jessie never took her eyes off the people who had just passed. Reed scanned the group. There were too many for him to pick out which one had excited his K-9.

Given the probability that someone nearby was carrying drugs, he wasn't too surprised. Even though Jessie wasn't trained to sniff out illegal substances, she had smelled them often enough on subjects she had tracked.

But that didn't mean he was on board with the uneasy feelings Jessie's behavior was bringing out. The sooner he picked up Midnight and returned to Abigail Jones's apartment, the better. For everybody.

As far as Abigail was concerned, Olga's presence was a plus. She would never have asked her friend to keep her company, but since she was already there, she hoped she'd stay.

The older woman emerged from the kitchen carrying two steaming mugs. "That one has a lot of nerve."

"He promised he'd be back."

"I hope he's happy. He made me miss my soap."

"We can watch it here," Abigail offered, blowing on the hot coffee before chancing a sip. "My cable box lets me run programs back to the beginning. You won't miss a thing." She reached for the remote. "What channel?"

"You want I should stay? I don't want to bother you."

"Yes, please. It's no bother. I—I don't like being alone all the time."

"So get yourself a fella," Olga said, taking the remote from her and quickly locating the correct TV channel. "Girl like you shouldn't have any trouble attracting a decent man." She smiled. "What about the one that just left?"

A shiver raced up Abigail's spine and prickled the nape of her neck. "I've seen enough bad relationships to stay away from all of them." She blushed. "I'm not letting any guy move in on me the way…"

"The way what?" Olga asked.

Abigail lowered her gaze. "The way my mother used to. That was almost as bad as her insisting I call every one of them Daddy." Embarrassed beyond words, she wished she hadn't spoken so bluntly. So truthfully. Yet now that she'd started to bare her soul she yearned to go on.

"What about your real papa?"

"I don't even remember what he looked like. My mother got mad at him once when I was little and destroyed every picture. I have nothing to remember him by."

"Did you ask her? Maybe she kept some for herself."

Shaking her head, Abigail took another sip before continuing. "I haven't seen Mama since I was sixteen. I have no idea where she even lives."

Olga began patting her free hand. "All right. I'll stay." She lifted her own mug as if in a toast to the soap opera. "Now we watch my show. I know some people say I'm foolish to want to see what happens, but you can learn a lot about life this way."

"I wish my life was as easy to understand," Abigail said softly. "I thought I was on the right track, helping homeless teens and doing good for society. Now I wonder."

"Nobody ever said doing the right thing was easy. That doesn't mean it isn't still right." Olga paused until the drama switched to a commercial, then said, "You keep the dog your friend is going to bring you, Mr. Rosenbaum will probably raise your rent."

Abigail hadn't thought of that but it fit with the way her days had been going lately. If it wasn't one thing, it was another. She had just about decided to tell Reed to take Midnight back where she came from when Olga added, "Of course, there's nothing like a big dog barking to scare off thugs." She chuckled. "Might not be such a bad idea after all."

Three flights of stairs and a frightened, gangly puppy were a bad combination, Reed mused, breathing hard as he carried wiggly, floppy, excited Midnight up to Abigail's. Before he had time to put his furry burden down, Jessie barked. The door was jerked open.

He set the pup on its big feet and smiled as he straightened. The look of astonishment on Abigail's face added to his amusement.

Eyes wide, she snapped her jaw closed and pointed. "That's a *puppy*?"

"Uh-huh. She's about five months old. They grow pretty fast at first."

"Yeah." Remaining in the doorway, Abigail held her hands apart to demonstrate something about the size of a domestic cat. "I was expecting, you know, a puppy. Little? Fluffy? Cuddly on my lap?"

"Midnight will cuddle you. Give her a chance."

Although she did step back, Reed could tell she was anything but sold on his idea even before she said, "All right. Come on in. But this is not going to work."

Jessie was first through the door and already on the couch by the time Reed was able to coax Midnight inside. Instead of compliantly trotting along on the end of the leash as she had at the training center and coming up the sidewalk from his SUV, she threw herself down, splayed out on her belly, and was sliding across the wood floor, inch by inch, while he tugged and cajoled. Astonishing! If she'd been trained to resist he'd have understood, but this was a puppy who was supposed to be leash-trained.

Abigail began to laugh. "Well, that's good if I need my floor dusted. What other tricks does she do?"

"She's pretty good at eating," Reed joked,

knowing he was blushing. "I promise you, she was behaving perfectly when I picked her up at the kennel and put the harness on her. This is very unusual. Working dogs need to be confident and unafraid."

"Maybe she senses my moodiness," Abigail offered. "Don't judge her by one incident. I'm sure she'll be fine once you take her back to where you got her."

"Mind if I catch my breath first? She wasn't crazy about climbing stairs, either."

Laughing, Abigail said, "What? A big, strong guy like you can't carry a puppy up three flights without getting winded? Does your chief know how out-of-shape you are?"

Reed started to argue, then realized she was teasing. "She was hard to hang on to," he said. "I almost dropped her a couple of times until I figured out she liked her front legs draped over my shoulder."

Abigail laughed again. "Can I get you a cup of coffee now, or would you rather have a sports drink?"

"Plain water's fine, thanks."

Eyeing Jessie and realizing the bloodhound wanted to follow Abigail, Reed unsnapped the pup's leash and gave Jessie a release command.

Off they went in Abigail's footsteps, one after the other, as if they were both tracking. Curiosity moved him to continue watching. He circled an easy chair and walked softly across the hardwood floor toward the kitchen.

What he observed was a Rockwell picture of Americana. Abigail was standing with her back to the refrigerator door, a bottle of cold water in each hand. The dogs were sitting politely at her feet, tails sweeping arcs on the floor, and acting as if their favorite human was about to serve the tastiest treats they'd ever eaten.

He waited to see what would happen. He wasn't disappointed. She began to speak to the dogs as though they were hers.

"What do you girls want, huh? A drink of water? I can probably manage that, but I'd better ask the officer first."

Jessie stayed in place. Midnight, excited by the kind tone of voice, wiggled and circled at Abigail's feet. Then she glanced over at her canine buddy and managed to resume a seated position without quivering too badly. The pup was smart, all right. She'd learned to beg after one impromptu lesson.

Waiting to see what happened next, Reed was startled by the loud ringing of a cell phone. He watched Abigail pale as she set the water bottles aside, reached for her phone and looked at the number. It must have been familiar because she quickly answered.

"Hello?"

Whatever the caller said caused her to lean against the counter. Was she shaking? Perhaps it was bad news and she needed moral support. Convinced he was right, Reed joined her and the dogs.

"I—I can't. I'm not ready," Abigail said, listening to the caller's reply before she added, "Are you sure?"

Apparently the answer was affirmative because her tight grip on the phone began to whiten her knuckles. He gently cupped her elbow and mouthed, "What's wrong?"

Distracted, she lowered the phone. Her eyes were wide and moist, her lower lip quivering slightly. "It's one of my kids. A girl I've been working with for several months. She insists she has to talk to me in person."

"Where?" Reed asked.

"She's at the AFS office where I work. That stands for A Fresh Start. It's only about six blocks away, right here in Brighton Beach. I usually walk, it's just that…"

"I understand. How about if we go with you?"

"You'd do that? Really?"

"Of course."

Abigail lifted the phone to her ear again and agreed to the rendezvous. "All right. I'll manage. Tell her to meet me there in thirty minutes."

Her blue eyes were still wide and misty when she ended the call and looked at Reed. "I hope that's enough time."

"It will be if we drive instead of dragging this pup on a leash. I'd like to see her relate to teens."

"Some of them are very troubled," Abigail told him.

"All the better for temperament testing."

"Right."

He saw Abigail standing very still and eyeing a purse that sat at the end of the kitchen counter. Clearly, she was far from over the trauma of nearly being abducted.

"Tell you what," Reed said, keeping his voice light and pleasant, "I'll go get my car and come pick you up. How does that sound?"

The smile she gave him showed great relief. "Sounds good. That way we won't have to drag Midnight and get her all dirty from the sidewalks."

He matched her smile with a wider grin. "I'll leave them both with you so Jessie can help influence the pup." After snapping short leashes on his K-9's collar and Midnight's harness, Reed handed the opposite ends to her. "You're in charge."

"Hey! Wait. I don't know what to do."

"It's easy. You just stand where you are or sit back down on the couch. They'll follow you."

"Like this puppy followed you up the stairs, you mean?"

Reed chuckled. His ploy had worked. Abigail was concentrating on handling the dogs instead of dwelling on her pending trip outside. Anything he could do to relieve her angst was a plus. It was likely that her healing would depend upon taking baby steps, such as initially venturing out with him as her companion and the dogs for distraction. She was certainly acting less afraid than she had when she'd first taken the phone call.

He gave Jessie the hand signal to stay, turned, and was almost to her door before Abigail called, "Hurry back."

That sounded so much better than the state in which he'd found her when he'd first visited, he was thrilled. The sooner she got over her fright and regained her memory of the incident at the carousel, the sooner the NYPD would be able to locate and arrest her assailants. At least, he hoped so. No matter how much he enjoyed the young woman's company, he was going to have to back off soon. His official duties didn't allow for much of a social life, not to mention the inadvisability of spending free time with the victim of a crime.

Jogging along the narrow sidewalk and dodging pedestrians, Reed realized he felt the absence of his K-9 partner. Jessie was so much a part of him, on and off duty, it was as if a critical element was missing. He could count times like this when he'd left her behind on the fingers of one hand.

The faster he moved the stronger his sense of foreboding grew. He had to get back to Abigail—and to Jessie—as fast as possible.

FIVE

Edging sideways toward the sofa, Abigail was surprised to find both dogs keeping her company the way Reed had promised. Once she was convinced they weren't going to go berserk, she began to relax a little and sat down. One of the dogs stepped on her toes. She didn't have to guess which one.

"I'm sorry, Midnight," she crooned like a mother to her baby, "this just isn't going to work out between you and me. You see that, don't you? Hmm? It's not that you're being difficult right now, it's just that I've never had a dog, let alone a puppy. I'd probably confuse you so badly you'd never become a police dog."

The pup's brown eyes sparkled, her ebony coat glistening. She wagged her whole rear end and panted at Abigail's feet, leaving a small damp spot on the right knee of her jeans. "See what I mean? Why can't you be still and easy to handle like Jessie is? Huh? Look how good she's being."

It took only a moment for Abigail to realize she'd goofed again by calling a name. Jessie, who had been calmly waiting at her feet, leaped onto the sofa next to her and took up the place she had chosen on her initial visit. That left Midnight alone on the floor, and it was clear she didn't intend to stay there when her canine companion was cuddling up to a friendly human.

Big, soft front paws landed in Abigail's lap as the puppy made an unsuccessful leap to join the party. Abby instinctively leaned forward and reached out to keep her from falling. She managed to hug the younger dog's shoulders, felt the texture of the glistening fur and received a wet slurp under her chin for her efforts.

"Eww! Stop," she ordered, chuckling in spite of herself. Rather than push Midnight back down she hoisted her onto the sofa on the side opposite Jessie. To say the pup was overjoyed was an understatement. It immediately crawled closer, succeeding in getting only its front half into her lap.

There was something very special about the unbridled attention and obvious acceptance of both dogs. When she'd been petting Jessie earlier, Abigail had thought she'd felt mild contentment. Having Midnight draped across her lap, gazing up at her and leaning that blocky head against her chest, was unbelievably comforting. Encircling the puppy in a gentle hug she stroked the velvety floppy ears and heard the youngster actually sigh. Who knew dogs could be so expressive?

Beside her, a growl rumbled in Jessie's throat. Was she jealous? Oh, dear. Now what?

"It's okay, Jessie," Abigail said quickly. "I love you, too."

That didn't placate the bloodhound. The quiet growl was followed by stronger rumbling, then a bark. Midnight's head whipped around. Both dogs were staring at the closed apartment door.

Abigail scooted forward to perch on the edge of the sofa, her body as still and tense as that of her canine companions. Something metallic was making a scratching sound. The doorknob was moving!

Before Abigail could decide what to do, Jessie began to give voice in a way that left no doubt she was extremely upset. Whoever was on the other side of that door was definitely not officer Reed Branson. And his K-9 partner knew it.

Finding a parking place directly in front of Abigail's apartment building was impossible, so Reed flipped on the blue-and-white Chevy

Tahoe's flashing lights and left it idling as close to already parked cars as possible.

He stepped out. Listened. Heard a dog barking. Traffic noise nearly drowned out Jessie's angry warning but the closer Reed got to the outer apartment door, the more sure he was. He slammed his palm into the bank of buttons on the intercom and was able to enter almost immediately because several residents responded.

Howling and guttural barking echoed down the stairwell, giving Reed's feet wings. He'd reached the second floor landing and was turning to start up to the third when a figure going the opposite direction bumped his shoulder so hard the blow nearly knocked him down!

Adrenaline enabled him to take the final section of stairway two and three steps at a time. He skidded to a stop at Abigail's door. Jessie was still barking. Puppy yips were background noise.

The hallway around him was empty. Reed knocked. "Abigail. Ms. Jones! It's me."

Not only did the dogs fall silent, it was quiet enough for him to hear her footsteps approaching. "It's really you?"

"Yes." He held his badge in front of the peephole. "See?"

Abigail opened the door and instead of ushering him in, threw both arms around his neck and fell into his embrace.

At their feet, Jessie was panting and wagging her tail. Midnight was so excited she ran in circles around the couple and wrapped their legs together with the trailing leash.

Reed braced himself against the doorjamb for balance. "Whoa. What happened? What's wrong?"

"I—I don't know."

"Okay. One thing at a time." He checked to make sure there was no immediate threat, then bent to unravel the snare of the short leash. "There. Let's go back inside."

Abigail didn't comply as quickly as he liked so he slid an arm around her waist and half carried her through the open doorway. Jessie entered ahead of them with the pup bringing up the rear, much to Reed's relief.

He closed the door, then escorted her to the sofa, sat down with her and clasped her hands. "All right. Tell me everything."

Although her blue eyes were wide and she still looked frightened, she said, "I think the dogs heard a prowler in the hallway. I—I heard a funny noise and thought I saw the doorknob turning but nobody came in."

"Not surprising considering the racket Jessie was making. She's not trained for personal protection but she knew she was supposed to look after you—and the puppy."

"Midnight barked, too. It would have been kind of cute if I hadn't been so scared."

"Well, there's no way we can prove someone was trying to break in," Reed said, choosing to keep his stairwell encounter to himself so Abigail wouldn't be as stressed. Reporting his suspicions to the 60th Precinct would suffice for now, since he had such a poor description of the possible suspect.

"Do you need a few more minutes or are you ready to leave?"

The emotions flashing across her pale, lightly freckled face came and went so fast Reed could hardly sort them out. Duty warred with fear. Where determination began and fright ended was less clear.

Abigail stared at him. "I promised I'd meet Kiera at the office. I have to go. How much time is left?"

"About ten minutes," he said cautiously. "Are you sure you're up to doing this?"

"No," she said with a tremor in her voice, "but I'm going to do it anyway."

He got to his feet and held out a hand to her. "Okay then. Let's get this show on the road."

"Dog," she said with a loud sigh.

"I beg your pardon?"

"This *dog* show. What in the world are we going to do with the puppy?"

The moment Reed's glance located Midnight he groaned. "Oops. I knew I should have walked her longer before I brought her in. I'll take care of your kitchen floor, then we'll take both dogs to my car and be on our way."

"Want to tell me again how much fun I'm going to have raising a half-grown pup?"

Speechless, he just rolled his eyes and hurried to take care of the housekeeping problem. Behind him he heard Abigail giggling. For a short time she had set aside her looming fear and was enjoying the moment. That relief was without price.

"You're double-parked!" Abigail was peering out through the glass fronting the foyer of her building.

"We do what we have to," Reed countered. "There was no place close by and I figured you'd appreciate a shorter walk."

"I do." She would have slipped her hand through the bend of his elbow if he hadn't needed both arms to carry the floppy pup.

"Okay, I'll go first with the dogs. Stick close behind me and you'll be fine."

"I'd rather carry Midnight and let you watch

my back," she said, trying to mask her growing unease.

"She's pretty heavy."

"I'm stronger than I look." Abigail extended her arms.

"All right. We want to make the trip to the car ASAP. Be careful going down the steps."

"Oof!"

"Told you she was a chunk."

"It's fine. I've got her." What she also had was the perfect opportunity to receive more doggie kisses, like it or not. "Eww. Why does she keep trying to lick me?"

"It's a pup's instinctive reaction to its mama. She's transferring her affection for Stella, her mom, to you."

"She thinks I'm her mother?"

"In a manner of speaking." Reed led the way to the SUV and opened the passenger side door, and Abigail climbed in, pup and all. One end of Midnight was on the center console, the other hanging off the right side of Abigail's lap.

"Give her to me and I'll put her in the back with Jessie."

"Can't she ride like this, with me?" She scooped up the rear of the gangly pup and gathered her long legs, tucking them under like the hem of a blanket.

"Not if we follow the law," he countered. "Being a cop is no excuse for rule breaking."

"I suppose not." Reluctance to let him take Midnight made her pull the pup into a bear hug, which resulted in more wiggling and expressions of joy from her furry burden.

Horns honked behind the idling SUV. Reed chuckled. "Okay. I'll put Jessie in the back, then come around and hook Midnight's harness to a seat belt. You fasten yours."

Abigail looked at her lapful, then at the clasp for the belt. "Sure. Easy-peasy. I'll do that with my extra two hands."

She heard Reed laughing as he let his bloodhound into the rear compartment, then slid behind the wheel and reached for the young Lab. Although Abigail tried to help by positioning Midnight for him, the entire operation was anything but smooth. By the time her harness was fastened everyone was breathing hard.

"Sorry," Abigail said. "The next time I'll let you put her in back with Jessie."

"I was just about to say the same thing." Reed shut off the flashers and signaled to pull into traffic. "Which way to your workplace?"

"Basically downtown Brighton Beach. Do you know where the open-air fruit and vegetable market is?"

Reed nodded.

"We're a couple doors past that. AFS leased a vacant storefront rather than pay exorbitant rent in an office building. Besides, we figured the kids we help would be more likely to wander into a place that looks less official. Know what I mean?"

"Absolutely. You need to use every trick in the book to bring them in."

"We're not tricking them," Abigail countered. "It's all about gaining their trust and providing aid without making them feel as if they have no choice."

"The way their parents treated them?"

She nodded slowly, pensively. "In some cases. Other kids come from situations that were so bad they feel they're better off wandering the streets with their friends. What they fail to see is how dangerous that lifestyle can be." A shiver zinged up her spine, reminding her to be cautious to the point of fear.

Sensing Reed's glance, she met it with her own eyes. "What?"

"I just saw you shiver. Are you okay?"

"I'm fine." *Just remembering being a lost kid myself,* she added silently. Traffic had slowed as they'd entered the old shopping section of Brighton Beach and she was relieved to have a reason to change the subject. She pointed. "There. See it? The sign in the window isn't very big, but that's the storefront."

"Got it. Want me to circle until I find a parking place or let you off?"

"Oh." That was a tricky question if she'd ever heard one. If she climbed out right there she could enter the A Fresh Start office quickly, but Reed and the dogs wouldn't be with her. If she insisted he park and escort her in, she might be late for her meeting with Kiera.

Abigail made a face at him. "I don't suppose you could do both, could you?"

"Sure. Hang on."

After angling into a narrow alley between buildings, he used his emergency lights again, circled the vehicle, got Jessie and met Abigail at the passenger door with a satisfied smile. "We'll walk you in, then I'll go park and come back for you."

Relieved, she asked, "What about my puppy? It's too hot to leave the poor little thing in the car."

One of his dark eyebrows arched and his grin widened. "What did you say?"

"Midnight." Abigail was frowning at him. "She can't stay in a hot car while we go inside." Climbing out to stand beside him and Jessie, she heard Midnight whining. "See what I mean? She doesn't want to be left behind."

"And if she got bored she'd probably rip the upholstery off any seat she could get her teeth into," Reed said. "I won't abandon her. I promise. This will only take a second and I'll lock her in with the AC running. Now let's get you inside for your meeting."

Abigail had already noticed how much more wary he was acting now that they were on foot. Good thing she hadn't been up to walking over from her apartment.

With Reed between her and Jessie, she hurried across the crumbling, cracked concrete sidewalk and ducked into her place of business. There were a few tattered posters taped to the walls, three old metal desks, a sofa with faded brown-and-gray upholstery and a couple of odd chairs. The well-used living room furniture was grouped in a back corner by a refrigerator to encourage more casual gatherings.

Abigail didn't see Kiera, but her boss, Wanda, greeted her with a smile. "I'm so glad you were feeling up to this. Kiera insisted she won't talk to anybody else."

"I understand. Where is she?"

"She didn't want to wait. I expect her back any minute." Wanda patted her on the shoulder. "Who's your friend?"

"This is…" She hesitated to give his job title where they might be overheard by prejudiced kids, so she merely said, "Reed." Smiling, she pointed. "And this is Jessie."

"We don't usually allow dogs in here," the slightly older woman said pleasantly, smoothing her bob and tucking longer strands of dark hair behind her ear on one side. "But in your case I may make an exception."

Flabbergasted, Abigail realized that her boss was flirting with the off-duty cop! She stifled a wry smile. *Well, well, well.* What a surprise.

"See you ladies again as soon as I go park," Reed said.

"I can comp your parking at the lot around the next corner if you want."

"No need. I'm just dropping off Ms. Jones for her meeting." He nodded politely and started to back away.

As he turned, his gaze caught Abigail's and she was sure she saw mirth twinkling in the rich depths. When he winked for her eyes only, she was positive.

Watching him saunter away with his K-9 partner was enough to dampen Abigail's joy. Yes, he would be back soon. And, no, she shouldn't be fearful doing the job she truly believed God had given her, yet she was. There were still too many unknowns lurking in the depths of her subconscious for her to fully relax in any situation, particularly one away from her apartment.

Before she had time to think herself into a snit, she spotted a familiar pierced and tattooed teenage girl with pink-fluorescent-streaked hair loitering outside the display window. Kiera had shown up.

Whatever was on the teen's mind was more important than Abigail's personal problems, she reminded herself. She'd faced her fears and braved the outdoors to get there. She wasn't going to blow a chance to offer the girl counseling.

If her memory didn't recover soon, maybe she'd take Reed's advice and see a professional herself. Remaining clueless indefinitely was unacceptable. And dangerous.

She clutched a file folder to her chest like a shield as the door opened and Kiera Underhill ducked through. The back of her long hair was gathered with an elastic band. She wore silver-and-pink chandelier earrings and a stud in her right eyebrow.

There had been a time when Abigail, herself, had delighted in marching to a different drummer, and she admired Kiera's spunk. What worried her was the teen's antagonistic attitude toward authority.

"Been there, done that," Abigail murmured, thinking back on the risks inherent in her own mistakes. If not for the grace of God and a few good influences at just the right times in her life, she wondered if she'd have survived to pass on the hard lessons she'd learned.

SIX

Abigail watched Kiera's approach and assessed her as nervous and perhaps deceitful. Well, that wasn't too surprising, given the girl's background. After being abused or abandoned or both, as in Kiera's case, it took time to heal.

No, *healing* was the wrong word, Abigail decided. It was more an adjustment of attitude and an acceptance of the mistakes of others, particularly one's parents. Some adults simply could not relate to the immature thought processes of a teen. Others had so many problems of their own they didn't even try to understand—or make the slightest effort at reconciliation with runaways. Those families produced the kids who were hardest to reach. They'd accept food and clothing and whatever else was offered but they never truly trusted. It wasn't in them.

Instead of the greeting Abigail had expected, Kiera sneered. "At least you showed up."

"I beg your pardon?" She faced the teen's ire

while Wanda made herself scarce, leaving the two of them essentially alone.

"Whatever," Kiera muttered. She bypassed Abigail and headed for the refrigerator. "Got any cold beer?"

"You know better than that."

"Yeah. I guess I'll have to settle for soda."

"Fine. Help yourself."

The teen not only did so, she threw herself backward into the center of the sofa and propped both feet on the scarred coffee table before she popped the top of the frosty can.

Displaying a good counselor's calm demeanor and posture, Abigail took the nearest chair, file folder on her lap, and leaned forward. "You wanted to talk to me?"

"Maybe."

Self-control had helped get her this job in the first place and she needed it now. She waited quietly, knowing that the more she probed, the more she urged the girl to open up, the less likely it was to happen.

"So," Kiera began, focusing on the soda can instead of her companion, "how are you?"

"I'm all right. Why?"

"Just wondered."

There was so much unsaid, Abigail felt unsteady, as if she were floundering in the waves that were ebbing, returning and breaking on the nearby shore. Her mind had suddenly made an unexpected jump and provided a startlingly clear image of a beach with storm clouds threatening. Just like the night she'd been attacked! She shivered, hoping the teen hadn't noticed.

Maybe Kiera hadn't, but Wanda had. She approached behind Abigail, laid a steadying hand on her shoulder and explained, "Ms. Jones was involved in a frightening attack down by the Coney Island boardwalk. She isn't feeling well but she came in today because you insisted you needed to speak with her. Please get to the point so she can go back home and rest."

The slim, tanned girl swung her feet to the floor and sat up straighter. "You were hurt? H-how? Did they…?"

"I just have a few bruises," Abigail assured her. "My main problem is my memory. I don't even know why I was over by Luna Park so late at night, let alone what happened to me, other than what I've been told."

"You—you don't?"

Abigail was getting the idea that Kiera knew more than she was telling. Speaking softly, she said, "No. Do you?"

"Naw. Not me." Kiera threw her body back against the sofa pillows again.

"Okay. So why did you want to speak with me today?"

"I don't. Not really." She lunged to her feet, splashing a few drops of the soda on her tank top. "Um, I gotta go."

Abigail saw Wanda start to intervene and held up a hand to signal her to stop. Obviously Kiera did know something about the incident in Coney Island. Her expressions and changes of mood gave her away, although she undoubtedly believed she was fooling the adults. That was all right. The time would come when she'd speak up. It almost always did when the runaway was kind-hearted behind a facade of bravado. Kiera wasn't a bad kid, she was just young and scared and trying to fight her way through to a better life with no idea how to go about it.

Kiera was on her way to the door, wasting no time, when Abigail called after her, "I expect to be back at work next week. Stop by anytime."

A raised soda can was the girl's only answer. She didn't even look back.

"What do you think is going on?" Wanda asked when they were alone.

"Maybe nothing, maybe plenty," Abigail said. "I got the idea she was fishing to find out what I knew. As soon as I admitted I couldn't remember what happened, she clammed up."

"I noticed. I'm surprised you let her get away with it."

"Right now, there's no way I can prove or disprove whatever she tells me," Abigail said with a sigh. "I sure wish I could remember at least a little about that night."

"You will," her boss said. "It just takes time. Do you really think you'll be ready to resume your duties by next week? That seems awfully soon."

"Pretty sure. Everybody keeps telling me it's not unusual for a brain to blot out trauma. I wish mine were not quite so efficient."

"Oh, I don't know," Wanda drawled. "If you stay the way you are, you'll probably have a lot more visits from your favorite cop."

Abigail's cheeks warmed and she knew her fair, freckled skin had begun to look sunburned even though it was not. "I never asked him to take an interest in my case. He says he's doing it because he was the one who found and rescued me and he feels some kind of divine assignment or something."

"Whatever works." Wanda was chuckling. "If you decide you're not interested, let me know." She nodded toward the front of the store. "Looks like he's still on volunteer guard duty."

The sight of Reed's back and broad shoulders through the glass made Abigail's pulse speed and stole breathable air from the surrounding atmosphere. How long had he been standing there? Had he seen Kiera leave? If so, why hadn't he come inside? Was he waiting until she gave him the okay?

Well, it was *very* okay for him to rejoin her, she decided easily. Being with Reed and the dogs gave her a morale boost as well as keeping her from jumping at shadows.

Abigail froze. *Shadows!* She remembered seeing shadowy figures. Trying to bring the hint of memory into focus, she closed her eyes and concentrated on the blurry picture. It was… It was gone.

Her shoulders sagged with disappointment. So close, yet still too far away, too buried in the labyrinth of her mind. Was seeing Kiera again the trigger? She supposed just getting out of her apartment and back into the office might have helped, too. So did Reed's presence, although she had yet to figure out why, other than equating it with him showing up at Luna Park after the attack.

It had been real. She was sure of that much. Bruises on her arms and wrists showed the patterns of large hands. Male hands. So one or more men must have grabbed her. Reed said his dog had alerted to screaming and her throat had hurt, so she figured the screamer had been her. And he'd found her hiding in the carousel control booth, another sign she'd been threatened.

Those facts were the bare bones of her ordeal.

In order to flesh it out and provide clues to the attackers, she was going to have to get past her nerves and unlock her mind. That was easier said than done. Until she remembered more details she didn't even know what questions to ask.

Thinking about this latest encounter with Kiera, however, she had a pretty good idea where to begin.

Reed glanced over his shoulder into the AFS office after he noticed a teenage girl leaving. Reflections of passing traffic and other pedestrians made it hard for him to see through the glass. He was about to approach the door when Abigail opened it and beckoned. Her serious expression turned to a smile when she noticed he'd brought both dogs this time.

As soon as Midnight spotted her, the tug-of-war was on. Reed had the pup's leash looped around his wrist, and her lunge toward Abigail pulled him sideways. A quick step and slight stagger set his balance right again. Some valiant defender he was, he mused. He must look like a flailing fool.

"Come on in. And bring your furry friends," Abigail said, chuckling, "before they flatten you."

"She caught me off guard, that's all. I can see she needs a lot more leash training."

"Will you show me how to do that?"

Reed pushed the door shut behind him and stepped farther into the office. "Seriously? Do you think you're ready to hit the streets with her?"

Good humor fled. "Well, no, but you can take her outside for me and I can walk her up and down the hallway for practice. That will help, won't it?"

"Sure, as long as you don't let her lead you. We're not sure of her strongest traits but she is headstrong."

"And so cute it's impossible to be mad at her. I'm not supposed to spank her, am I?"

"No. Absolutely not. That could make her afraid of all human contact and she needs to use her brain to tell the good guys from the bad guys."

"Police dogs really do that?"

"All dogs do to some extent," Reed said. "The secret is teaching them proper responses." He nodded to Wanda before turning his concentration back to Abigail. "So, what did the girl want to tell you that was so urgent?"

She shrugged. "Beats me. Kids like Kiera are masters at avoidance, but her body language gave me the idea that she may have seen what happened to me down by the boardwalk."

The short hairs at the back of Reed's neck prickled. "What makes you think that?"

"Her attitude, mostly. And the way she changed the subject when I asked her if she knew anything about it." Abigail sighed audibly. "I am sure she was worried I'd been hurt because she asked me. That's a positive sign. She does have a tender heart, she's just learned to hide those feelings, and it's going to take more than one meeting to convince her she should share information. Maybe she heard rumors from some of the other kids. I don't know."

"Okay." Reed shortened the puppy's leash to keep her close to his side and inclined his head toward the door. "Let's get you home and settled in again, then I'll go by headquarters and check up on her via computer. Do you know if she has a juvenile record?"

"I don't think so. I haven't known her for very long. There's a tremendous turnover in kids who hang out at the beach in the summer. Most have homes to go to and unless they show a need or happen to drop in here with friends, it's hard to tell much about them."

"How do you know they aren't scamming you?"

That question brought a sweet, pensive expression to Abigail's face. "We don't. We do check, of course, but getting their real names is tough enough, let alone the true story of their past. It takes time to develop rapport and some are only here for a short time. Foot traffic dies down in the winter."

"I imagine so. Do you take them in if the weather turns bad?"

"We don't, but we have connections with some of the area churches and other charities that do. I'd never let my kids suffer on the streets."

That statement, her owning of the lost children, struck Reed as the crux of her personality. She was a nurturer. Oh, she might not know it or might deny it if asked, but that was what she was. Everybody's mother. The other notion that stuck in his mind was wondering how such a young, seemingly fragile woman had developed the inner strength to carry off the daunting task of tending to a myriad of ungrateful strangers, week after week, year after year.

When—if—he got to know her better, he might even ask.

Abigail managed to leave A Fresh Start without too much angst because of Reed and the dogs. At first she felt hesitant, but as they walked toward the lot where he had left his car, she began to actually enjoy the brisk day. Temperatures had moderated since the storm the night of her attack and the weather was about as perfect as fall along the Atlantic could get. Some seagulls whirled overhead while others, and smaller birds, squabbled over bits of food in the street and along the curb.

"That reminds me," Reed said, "are you hungry? I'll buy."

His offer startled her. Under other circumstances she might have been flattered, but eating out would mean a delay in getting back to her apartment and was therefore unacceptable.

"Sorry. No," she said too quickly.

"I'm the one who should apologize for asking," he told her. "You seemed so calm I thought you might be up to it."

"I am better. Who wouldn't be on such a beautiful day? But I still feel as if I'm being watched."

"Why didn't you say so?"

Abigail huffed a chuckle. "And convince you I'm paranoid? I don't think so." She concentrated on watching the dogs rather than meet his gaze. Thinking about the weather and the birds and the dogs had distracted her some, but it hadn't taken much to pull her back into survival mode. There was no way she was even close to being normal.

The crush of pedestrians around them, the noise of traffic, the calls of vendors and incessant chatter along the busy street were drowning Abigail in sensory stimuli. Everything pressed in on her as if she were being swamped by a tsunami of sound or lost in a forest of trees so close together there was no clear avenue of escape.

"My car is right around the next corner," Reed said. "Do you think you can take charge of Midnight for a bit until I get Jessie loaded?"

A nod was all she could muster. He handed her the leather leash and she slipped her hand through the end loop. Reed's concern was evident. If there had been a way to explain how rapidly a sense of looming disaster had overcome her, she would have done so. Gladly. All it had taken was a simple question and she was headed straight over a figurative cliff again. There had to be a way to stop these panic attacks. There had to be. Because if she failed to get control of her own emotions she wasn't going to be fit to help anyone else.

It was one thing to study human behavior in school and quite another to apply that knowledge to her personal life, let alone those of others. Head knowledge didn't erase irrational fear any more than wishful thinking did.

So, what options did she have? Abigail asked herself. Wanda would cite total reliance on faith and prayer, she knew, and if that had ever worked well for her in the past, she might consider it. Night after night she'd prayed that her father would return and that her mother would stop partying and bringing home strange men, yet nothing had changed. Inevitably, she had run away and become a street kid just like the ones she was now trying to aid.

Abigail froze as her thoughts came full circle. The unanswered prayer had forced her to leave, sent her into the streets and eventually to school, where she became qualified to do what she was currently doing for others. If God had given her the results she'd prayed for, who knew where she'd have ended up or what she'd be doing for a living?

Looking back, she suddenly realized she was acting like a foxhole Christian, only praying when she was out of other options or too scared to think straight. No wonder she assumed God wasn't listening. The only time she called on Him was during an imminent disaster.

Like the assault, she added, stunned by the recollection.

A sharp intake of breath drew Reed's attention. He wheeled. "What is it? Did you see somebody?"

"No." Although she was a bit breathless, she nevertheless explained. "I just remembered something I did the other night before you found me."

"Running? Hiding? Getting grabbed?" he asked, finishing loading his K-9 and stepping closer to Abigail.

She shook her head. "No. Praying."

Instead of congratulating her on bringing back a lost fact, Reed began to smile. Seeing that was disconcerting enough for her to ask, "What's so funny?"

"Not funny. Gratifying," he drawled. "It feels good to be the answer to someone's prayers."

"How do you know you are?"

The self-satisfied smile grew into a grin. "Because you probably asked for help and I was sent. Go ahead. Deny it."

She sighed and shook her head. "I don't remember what I prayed for. I just thought it was a good sign that I recalled doing it."

"It's always good," he countered, loading the puppy into the secure second seat space, then opening the front passenger door for her.

As she slid in and reached for her seat belt, she was frowning. "Which one? Praying or remembering an inconsequential detail like that?"

"Talking to God is never inconsequential," Reed admonished gently. "Answers always come in one form or another. All we have to do is accept them when they come and recognize how blessed we are."

She waited until he slid behind the wheel before she said, "It's never worked that way for me."

"Sure it has." Reed started the SUV and merged into traffic. "You just haven't been looking with your heart."

Mentally working on a logical argument, Abigail saw something flash in her peripheral vision. She tensed. Opened her mouth to warn Reed of the anomaly.

It was too late. A white box truck sped out of nowhere and smashed into the side of the SUV with a rending of metal and shattering of glass.

Abigail gasped, intending to scream, but the air was knocked out of her by the impact. Her seat belt grabbed her chest and kept her from being thrown across the front seats.

They were sliding sideways into oncoming traffic. She threw her arms across her face and braced for a second impact as the airbags exploded.

SEVEN

It had taken Reed a split second to realize there was no way to take evasive action. Even if he had seen the danger long before they were hit, he couldn't have maneuvered out of the way. A box truck had left the alley accelerating, tires squealing, and had smashed into the Chevy Tahoe before he'd had time to even brace himself.

Glass had shattered from the impact. They slid across the street into oncoming traffic and barely missed connecting with a city bus before jumping the curb and coming to rest against a power pole. Thankfully, their speed had slowed enough by then to keep that damage to a minimum.

Reed shouted. Abigail screamed. Around them, cars bumped each other like a line of toppling dominoes.

He'd felt the seat belt bruising his ribs as he'd mashed down the brake with all his strength. It was hard to let up once the vehicle came to rest but he knew he had to.

"Are you all right?" he shouted to Abigail.

"I—I think so. I saw the truck coming but I didn't have time to warn you."

"It wouldn't have mattered." As the airbags collapsed he was able to reach the ignition and shut off the engine, then key his radio and identify himself before saying, "I'm ten-fifty-three H. Hit and run. Just got T-boned by a white box truck that is now headed west on Surf Avenue."

"Copy," the dispatcher radioed back. "License?"

"Didn't get it," Reed replied with disgust. "I had a face full of airbag."

"Copy that. Injuries?"

"Negative, as far as I know, but I'm not the only one hit. It's going to take half the cops in Brighton Beach to sort out this mess."

"Affirmative. Units on the way."

He unfastened his seat belt and swiveled to face Abigail. "You're sure you aren't hurt?"

She was brushing off crystal-shaped bits of tempered glass. "My shoulder is kind of sore, that's all."

"Probably from the belt or the airbag," he explained. "Anything else? Did you hit your head?"

"No. How about you?"

"I'm fine."

Her voice rose. "Oh, no! What about the dogs?"

"I'll go check them. You stay put while I try to convince all these motorists that the police are on their way and there's no need to fight over who's to blame."

"I'll tell them it wasn't your fault," she vowed. Her fingertips brushed Reed's forearm as he left the damaged vehicle, sending a spark of awareness racing along his nerves.

How like Abigail to think of others first. Most of the women he knew, and half the guys, would be complaining their heads off. She, however, was concerned about him and the dogs.

Circling, Reed opened the hatchback and began to examine both dogs. Neither seemed injured but the pup was trembling in fright. He leashed Jessie first, then Midnight, and brought them around to Abigail while bystanders jostled and pushed past each other to capture everything on their cell phone cameras. It would be too much to hope that one of the onlookers had taken pictures of the truck that hit him, but he'd have incoming officers check anyway. Judging by the lights and sirens pulling up to the snarl, he'd have plenty of help.

The passenger door was caved in, its mechanism jammed, so Reed spoke to Abigail through the shattered side window. "See if you can slide out the other door without getting cut on this broken glass. If you can't get over the console, I'll have the fire department pry this side open."

"I think I can do it." She managed a lopsided smile. "If I can stop shaking long enough."

She wasn't the only one, he admitted to himself. It might not show on the outside but his guts were churning. Was it possible that the truck had hit them on purpose? The more he thought about it, the more he wondered.

A bigger question was, who was the target? His K-9 unit had suffered its share of attacks lately, beginning with the unsolved murder of Chief Jameson. It was possible the truck driver had seen the logo and had smashed into the blue-and-white SUV because he hated cops, especially K-9 ones.

On the other hand, Reed speculated, the passenger side had taken the hardest hit. Abigail's side. Anybody who had watched them walk back to the parking lot would have known who was on board with him and which seat she was occupying. Plus, this was her home turf. Perhaps her sense of ongoing menace wasn't all in her imagination.

He hurried back to the driver's door to help her climb out, then shepherded her onto the sidewalk before handing her both dogs' leashes.

"Stay right here. You'll be safe. I need to go speak with the arriving officers."

The pleading look in those blue eyes nearly undid him. When she asked, "Do you have to?" Reed knew instantly that he wasn't going anywhere. Not until he'd arranged for a policewoman to stay with her.

"No," he said tenderly, "we can let them come to us."

When she sighed softly and sagged back against the side of the brick building where they stood, it was all he could do to keep from taking her in his arms and offering comfort.

Instead, he displayed his badge for the patrolman who was working his way through the crowd, clearly searching for the wreck's driver.

As the throng parted, Reed noticed two people in particular who weren't acting interested in the wreck, the dogs or the police presence. One was heavy and wearing a baseball cap while the other was thinner and peering between taller spectators. Clenching his jaw, he stared at them, then took out his cell phone, intending to photograph their faces.

By the time he held it up and zeroed in on the place where they had been, they had melted into the crowd. He lowered the phone and searched for them, deciding that they must have separated.

Abigail touched his shoulder, distracting him for the millisecond it took to lose track of the bigger guy in the baseball cap. Since he had nothing to show her, he chose to keep the incident to himself. But he wouldn't forget those men. They'd been standing stock-still, glaring directly at Abigail.

If Abigail had not had two loving, attentive canines at her feet and a policewoman close by, watching, she figured she'd have lapsed into hysterics long before she and Reed were allowed to leave the site of the wreck.

So weary she was almost tempted to sit on the dirty sidewalk, she perked up when she saw him approaching. The smile on his face was a plus. "Can we leave?"

"Yes, as soon as I transfer my gear to the replacement vehicle my unit is sending." He inclined his head toward the smashed SUV. "I broke that one."

"Not by yourself. You had help."

"No kidding. That's why they want to tow it even if it's drivable. Crime scene techs need to go over it before it's repaired and put back in service."

Many locals had lost interest in the scene and drifted off, leaving the sidewalk fairly clear. Firefighters were rolling up hoses they'd positioned as standby. Someone with an impressive-looking camera and an NYPD jacket was circling the scene and snapping photo after photo. A tow truck driver was hooking his implements to the rear bumper of the wreck.

Abigail did feel a little calmer by then, but she wasn't through being edgy. The hair on her arms and the back of her neck was prickling as if she were sunburned despite standing in the shade of the brick building.

Surprisingly, Reed scowled. "What's wrong? Are you hurt after all?"

She shook her head. "No. Why? Do I look that bad?"

"I can have an EMT from the fire department look you over. It's no big deal." The frown deepened. "Tell me the truth."

"I am telling you the truth. I wasn't hurt. It's just…"

Reed stepped closer, scanning their surroundings and finding nothing amiss. "Just what?"

"Nerves." Her voice wasn't as self-assured as she would have liked, but there was nothing she could do about it.

"Understood. I should have had one of the other officers take you home earlier. Sorry."

"I probably would have argued with you then, but it has been a long day." She was scanning the street. "Look. Is that the car we're waiting for?"

"Yes. About time, too." Stepping off the curb, he flagged down an SUV identical to his. It pulled over and he leaned in the passenger side window. Abigail trailed after him, surprised to see a grinning uniformed woman behind the wheel. A closer look told her the pretty brunette was also a K-9 cop. And she was taunting Reed.

"That's some fender bender, Branson. You plan to polish out the dings on your lunch hour?"

Reed huffed. "It's gonna take a lot more than elbow grease to fix that mess." He noted Abigail's arrival over his shoulder and made introductions. "Brianne, this is Ms. Jones. Abigail. She was the victim of an incident that Jessie and I worked at Coney Island a few nights ago."

"And…?"

"And, she'll be fostering one of Stella's pups for us. The sweet one that was returned after failing the initial assessment for police work."

"Let's hope she can still become a service dog." Looking past Reed, she said, "Nice to meet you, Abigail. I take it you have the necessary experience?"

"Well, I…" Lying was wrong, yet she loved the puppy already and did want to keep her.

"I'm going to be assisting until Ms. Jones is well prepared," Reed said. "So, how is Stella coming along?"

"Fine. Don't change the subject. Has this placement been approved by Noah?"

"He approved a trial placement," Reed informed Brianne. "Now, if you're ready I'll load the dogs and we'll drop you at headquarters."

"Won't be necessary," the other K-9 officer said, leaving the SUV. "I'll catch a ride in one of the patrol cars." She cast a sidelong glance at Abigail and raised her eyebrows. "Wouldn't want to cramp your style, Branson."

"It's not like that," Reed insisted. "This is community service. And I'm on my own time."

"If you say so." By the time Brianne started to turn away, she was grinning.

Concerned, Abigail followed Reed around to the rear in case he needed her to help. "I don't want to get you in trouble."

"Don't mind her. All cops tend to be cynical. If it looks suspicious, it probably is. That doesn't mean she's right. My boss understands why I brought Midnight to you."

"Something tells me it wasn't only for the dog's sake."

"What difference does it make? We need good foster homes and you can provide one. If you happen to get personal benefit from the placement, it's win-win."

"I don't want to do anything wrong."

"Let me worry about that, okay? Now climb

in. I was starving before we were attacked and—"

"We were what? I thought this was an accident." She could tell by his expression that he hadn't meant to reveal so much.

Once she got that notion in her head, it was impossible to erase it. If the truck slamming into them was trying to hurt them, then the whole incident began to make sense. It had zoomed out of that alley so fast she'd barely had time to gasp, let alone shout a warning to Reed. Yes, New Yorkers had a reputation for aggressive driving, but entering traffic so carelessly wasn't something a delivery driver would do if he wanted to keep his job.

"I never looked at the faces of the people in the truck," she said ruefully. "Maybe if I had, I'd have gotten over my temporary amnesia and recognized them."

"Or maybe they had a beef with all cops and wanted to take one out," Reed countered. "You can't be sure they intended to hurt you."

"Hurt me?" Abigail gave an ironic-sounding chuckle. "If it was connected to the attack in Luna Park, I suspect somebody wanted to do more than just hurt me. Those people don't know my memory is gone so they probably believe I can ID them for whatever they've done."

She swallowed hard. "I think they hoped to permanently eliminate the threat. Namely, me."

Reed didn't say much during the drive back to Abigail's apartment, but his brain provided plenty of opinions regarding the accident.

Getting a large truck into position to smack into the passing police vehicle would have been iffy at best, yet the notion that the seeming attack had been a real accident was hard to swallow. Taking the incident at face value was foolish. It might give him ulcers to keep assuming the worst, but that was the only way to stay on guard against a surprise attack. This afternoon was proof of that.

He'd been having a nice time playing escort for Abigail Jones. Too nice. And he had overlooked impending danger. Whether their attackers had meant bodily harm or not, it was unsettling to be the bull's-eye of anyone's target. He sure didn't want to have a working police K-9 named after *him* posthumously like his partner, who represented fallen officer Jessie Ramirez.

Deep in thought, Reed was jarred when Abigail reached across and touched his arm. "I'm sorry."

"For what?"

"For dragging you over to Brighton Beach and getting your car wrecked."

Reed was shaking his head as he glanced at her. "Don't be ridiculous. You didn't force me to go anywhere. That was my idea. And you weren't driving, I was, so the responsibility for the accident rests on me. Period."

"You said it wasn't an accident."

"It will be looked into. Nobody is sure the truck was after us."

"But they drove away."

"Maybe they had criminal records. Or maybe their cargo wasn't legit, and they didn't want it checked. There are plenty of reasons why people dodge the law."

Tears glistened in her eyes. "That's true, I suppose."

"Of course it is. This job, this life, is not for everyone. It can alienate you from friends and family, for one thing." Pondering his own past, he began to smile. "When my dad was trying to talk me out of going to the police academy, he used to say I'd be making myself the skunk at the Sunday school picnic."

"That's terrible."

"But it can be valid," Reed said pensively. "Dad was being realistic. Civilian attitudes toward cops aren't always complimentary." A red light stopped them, giving him time to study her expression in more depth. She looked slightly distressed, but unless he missed his guess, there was a lot more emotion boiling beneath her surface of pseudo-calm.

When she said, "You don't have to be a cop to get ostracized—it can happen to anybody whose ideas conflict with the latest public whims," her expression gave him confirmation.

"What somebody else decides is their right even if it's against the law," he added.

Abigail was slowly nodding. She'd averted her face, but he could see her reflection in the side window's glass. It looked as if her cheeks were wet with tears.

"That's the hardest part," she said quietly. "Sticking to your principles when you know other people are doing wrong. It's especially hard for kids like the ones I help."

"You must be good at your job for a tough teen like Kiera to want to confide in you," Reed told her. "I can tell you have empathy. That's a special gift."

Her head snapped around and she stared at him. "A gift?" She huffed. "It's more like the scar from a horrible wound, one I will never forget."

EIGHT

There was no parking available in front of her apartment building. Abigail said, "Stop and let me out here."

"You want me to walk you in, don't you?"

Yes, she did. And *no*, she was not going to admit it. Not after letting down her guard and revealing too much personal information. After unsnapping the seat belt, she used her shoulder to nudge open the door, then slid out. The polite thing to do would be to invite Reed in, but at that moment she was so disgusted with herself she simply wanted to be alone. No people. No dogs. If she let their camaraderie resume he was bound to start asking personal questions. Questions she did not want to answer.

"I can manage fine by myself." The keys to the foyer door and her apartment were on a ring tucked into the pocket of her jeans opposite her cell phone. Fishing out the keys, she left the street and hurried up the stone steps.

A sidelong peek showed that Reed was getting out of the car. "Hey! Wait for me."

Abigail's fingers were trembling as she tried to hold the first key steady. Noise in the street was making her head swim. What was wrong with that key? It had always fit easily into the lock before.

A car backfired. She jumped as if it were a gunshot. *Key, key. Come on.* Grabbing her right hand with her left, she managed to control the action enough to unlock the street door and step through. The automatic locking mechanism clicked into place behind her.

Fisting the key ring, she started up the stairs. By the time she reached the first landing she was running. Panting. Gasping. Hoping and praying to reach her apartment before her burst of nervous energy gave out. The sense that someone was pursuing her was strong and growing. That was ridiculous in the secure building, of course, but it didn't keep her imagination from insisting otherwise.

"Why didn't I let Reed come up with me?" she kept asking herself. "Why?" Was it false pride? Fear that he would look down on her if he knew the whole truth? Or had she somehow reverted to the frightened, lost teen she'd been when she'd fled her home and sought solace on the streets with others of her kind, throwaway kids nobody cared about or missed enough to look for?

Reaching the third floor, Abigail hurried to 312, managed to use the key and darted inside, slamming the door behind her and turning the dead bolt for extra security. Home. Sanctuary. Peace and quiet.

She leaned against the inside of the door, catching her breath and struggling against the panic, before she actually looked at her living room. There was a beige sofa and coordinating frieze on an occasional chair. Silk flowers waited in a milk glass vase atop a small dining table at the end of the kitchen, and the portion of the counter that was visible was tidy.

So why was she still sensing a threat? She folded her arms across her chest and studied the apartment as if she were a CSI looking over a crime scene.

Throw pillows? Check. Curtains pulled to dim the light from outside? Check. Library book on the end table by the chair? Check. Daily mail? Uh-oh. She began to scowl. "I'm sure Olga put it on the table when she brought it up for me." Was it possible she had merely imagined the daily routine happening again? And where was her purse?

Abigail's chest tightened with a band of tension that again restricted her breathing. She'd taken her purse to work with her. It was either still at the office or in the K-9 cop's wrecked vehicle! If that SUV ended up in a repair garage, there was no telling what would become of her personal property.

Her cell phone was cradled in her hand before she realized she hadn't saved Reed's number. Dialing 911 as if her problem was an emergency was wrong, so what other options did she have? She wasn't even sure he was connected to the precinct that patrolled her neighborhood.

Feeling guilty for calling out to God only when she was in dire straits, Abigail nonetheless prayed, "Lord, what now?"

Instead of receiving a sense of calm, she thought she heard an unfamiliar noise. She held her breath. Listened for it to repeat. Had it come from her bedroom? Walls between apartments weren't soundproof, so it could have come from next door. But what if it hadn't? Instinct insisted she should turn around and leave.

"And go where?" she said, barely speaking and relying on the sound of her own voice for slight solace. The deserted hallway could be just as menacing as what she thought she'd just heard. Suppose her imagination was on overload again?

Abigail pressed her back against the inside of her entry door. Reed had told her he'd seen at least two men leaving the scene of her assault, so what if one was in there with her and the other waited in the hall?

The phone in her hand vibrated! She fumbled with it, trying to answer. Instead of hello, she whispered, "Help," then hoped the call wasn't from a telemarketing computer.

"Abby? Abigail? Are you all right?"

It was Reed. *Praise the Lord*, it was Reed.

"Why did you run off? What's going on?"

Her mouth was so dry she could hardly speak. Cradling the phone, she cupped her other hand around her mouth and said, "I think there's somebody in the apartment with me."

"I'm already on my way. Hide!" he shouted in her ear.

Abigail would gladly have followed his orders if she could have. Unfortunately, her body was refusing to listen to her mind. Her sandals might as well have been nailed to the living room floor.

An interior door shut with a *snick*.

Abigail willed herself to flee. Nothing happened.

Footsteps made a slow, unmistakable cadence.

She inhaled. Swallowed a gasp. Watched for signs of the prowler she was now certain of. Her head was swimming. Her stomach lurched. Tight fists made her nails cut into her palms.

That pain was enough to jar her loose. She dropped to the floor and crawled behind the sofa. Heartbeats in her ears mimicked a bass drum. Intakes of breath were like a hurricane. Evil filled the atmosphere.

She held her breath as best she could and waited. There were no words for another divine supplication. All she could do was picture Reed Branson and pray in her heart that he reached her in time.

If Reed had taken the time to park before phoning Abigail's cell, it might have taken him longer to respond. As it was, he'd made up his mind to join her whether she liked it or not. That decision had supposedly been based on delivering Midnight, but he wasn't fooling himself. He wanted, he needed, to see with his own eyes that she was all right.

And now he knew otherwise. No wonder something inside him had kept insisting he must not leave her. She was in trouble. And it was her own fault. If she hadn't jumped out of the car and taken off he'd have been there to help her.

The staircase to the third floor was deserted this time. Breathing hard, he tried the knob on her door. It didn't turn. Should he knock and tip off a possible prowler or smash in the door and take a chance on traumatizing Abigail?

He knocked. "Ms. Jones?"

Nothing.

He rapped louder. "Abigail?"

TV and movie cops broke down doors with their shoulders. Real ones knew better. Lacking a battering ram and sufficient manpower to swing it, he readied himself for a kick.

The knob moved. Reed put a hand on the butt of his concealed .38, ready to draw if necessary.

Then he heard her whisper his name. "Reed?"

The door swung open. Abigail was standing there, tears streaming down her face, cheeks pale, hair mussed, looking more like one of the street kids she helped than she did a social worker.

Every muscle in his body was taut, his nerves primed. "You okay?"

She nodded, then stepped back and pointed to the hallway he hadn't explored when he'd visited before.

"The prowler?"

"Yes. I heard him back there."

This time, Reed did draw his weapon. Thumb resting on the safety, he gestured to Abigail with his free hand. "You stay here." Her lack of positive response made him hesitate. "I mean it. Don't move till I get back."

"O-okay."

There were only two doors off the short hallway and both of them were open. A tiny bathroom had no outlet. Her bedroom, however, had a window that provided access to a fire escape. Sea breezes were lifting the leading edges of the curtain.

Reed paused only long enough to make sure the prowler hadn't set a trap by hiding in the closet, then hurried to the open window and looked down the fire escape. A large person wearing a dark hoodie dropped down from the extension ladder and hit the sidewalk running.

"Police! Freeze!" Reed shouted, figuring his chances of compliance were zero to none. He was right. The fleeing man had a nondescript car waiting and disappeared into it.

Holstering the .38, he returned to Abigail. She had obviously recovered some but was still far from sedate. "Sorry," Reed told her, "he got away."

"Did you see him?"

"Not enough to identify. He ran down the fire escape. I'll have the window frame dusted for prints but I doubt we'll find any."

"I always keep that window closed and locked."

He nodded and began investigating the rest of the apartment. "I'm glad I got here before he had a chance to harm you. Can you tell if he stole anything?"

"There's hardly anything in here worth stealing," she replied. "I live simply. My computer is at work and I keep a tablet in my purse. Which reminds me. I think I left the purse in your wrecked car. I really need it."

"Understood." Search completed, he studied her. Whether she realized it or not, she couldn't stay here. Not until she remembered enough for the police to recognize and capture her enemies. The question was, how was he going to convince her to find a more secure place to live when he knew she considered her current apartment a sanctuary?

Perhaps being blunt would save them all time and argument. "You need to find some other place to stay for a little while," Reed said flatly. "Call a friend."

All Abigail did was shake her head.

"I'm serious. You can't stay here now that we know how vulnerable you are."

"New York is full of burglars. I'll keep the window locked."

"I thought you said you already did."

"Well, he must have jimmied it." Beginning to pace, she waved her hands in the air as proof of her frustration. "I don't know."

Reed leaned back against the kitchen counter, folded his arms and gave her a steady look. "Think for a minute. The locks on the window are fine. I just checked. It seems more likely that he got in through the door and used the window for a quick exit when he heard me coming."

Rosy color drained from her face. Her lips parted. Her eyes widened, glistening. "How?"

"Our crime scene techs may have some idea after they've examined this place, but don't count on it. Old buildings are covered with scars." Waiting for her to come to a suitable conclusion was driving him crazy, so he stepped closer and clasped her upper arms gently. "Look, I know none of this is your fault, but that doesn't make it any less real. The more disturbing events pile up on you, the less likely you are to be able to recover your memory. That alone should be enough to convince you to move."

"I don't have any place to go."

"Friends?"

"Not any with extra room."

"How about the lady downstairs. Olga? She'd probably take you in."

"No way. I'd be putting her in jeopardy. The same goes for my boss, Wanda."

A solution to the problem had occurred to him already and he had discarded it for several reasons, not the least being his inconvenient attraction to this young woman. If—and that was a big if—he ever did decide to marry and settle down, his wife would need to be strong-willed and stable emotionally in order to cope with the trials and rigors of a cop's job. Abigail Jones was far too sensitive and empathetic for a life like that.

The arrival of patrol officers distracted Reed for the next ten minutes. By the time those men had spoken with Abigail he'd made up his mind. With nothing stolen and no harm to the occupant of the apartment, nothing would be done about this invasion of her privacy. That left only one alternative as far as he was concerned. He'd have to take her home to Rego Park, Queens, with him.

Reed grimaced. His sister, Lani, was not going to be happy about sharing her half of their place. Not happy at all. The only element of his idea that might appeal to her was taking in Midnight as well as Abigail Jones. Lani was a sucker for dogs. After all, she was also becoming a part of their K-9 unit and had never met a dog she didn't love.

That way the pup could learn manners from watching an older dog. He smiled to himself. Talk about coming up with the perfect excuse to include the young Lab. He was a genius! There was no way Lani could refuse to go along with his idea when there was a needy puppy involved.

NINE

All Abigail wanted after the stressful morning she'd had was to kick off her shoes and stretch out on the sofa. Instead, she had company that kept needling her. "I still don't see how sharing a place with you and your sister is better than staying here. Don't you both work?"

"Yes, but not necessarily the same shifts. Besides, nobody will know where you've gone."

"It's not practical. Queens is too far from my kids."

"I get it. I do," Reed said, "but I can arrange to drive you back to this neighborhood. It's not as if Rego Park is out of state."

Her glance drifted over the inanimate objects in her living room. Nothing she owned held particular importance for her. Resale shops had provided the furniture, tag sales the kitchenware and bargain stores the incidentals. It was all generic and nothing had been a gift.

The only photos she had displayed on the

bookcase were of a few of the kids she had pulled in off the streets and rehabilitated. Many others had refused to let her take their pictures. She understood why. Life had damaged their capacity to trust, especially with regard to adults, and they didn't want to leave behind any clue to themselves, no matter where they went after leaving Brighton Beach.

She could identify with them. When she had run away and stayed on the streets during her sixteenth summer, she had acclimated far more than she had expected. If it hadn't been for a mentor, a woman like she had become, there was no telling how far she might have sunk and whether she would have even lived this long. Given that she was essentially paying back a debt to the loving group that had saved her from destruction, she couldn't knowingly throw it all away through false pride or stubbornness. She had to yield to Reed.

"All right," Abigail said, turning to him. "Call your sister and make sure she doesn't mind if I camp there for a little while. If it's okay with her, I'll go."

"She's fine with it."

Studying his ruggedly handsome face she half smiled. "You haven't asked her, have you?"

"Well, no, but I know Lani. She won't mind. And having a yard for the pup is a big plus. Otherwise you'd have to take her out and walk her on the street half a dozen times a day. You don't want to do that, do you?"

Abigail huffed. "I already agreed to go. You can save the big sell."

"Yes, ma'am." Reed was grinning at her.

"I do appreciate all you've done for me. I don't know anyone else who would have used so much of his free time for the benefit of a stranger."

"You're not a stranger," he countered. "Not anymore. Grab whatever you think you'll need and let's go. The dogs are waiting."

"I can't believe you left them both in the car," she said, intending to sound critical.

"I told you the AC was on. They were secure and fine. Did you expect me to take the time to get them out and lug that moose up the stairs when I knew you were in trouble?"

"No." She made a face. "You're right."

"Well, that's an improvement."

One eyebrow arched higher than the other and she tilted her head to the side. "What is?"

"You just said I was right about something. I may keel over from shock any minute."

"Hey, if I have an opinion, you're going to hear it, regardless."

Reed had to chuckle. "No kidding."

Hands fisted on her hips, Abigail took a stand in more ways than one. "Look. I know I've been traumatized. I'm not my usual self, nor am I the person you met at Luna Park. I'm no helpless weakling. I've had to fight to be taken seriously all my life and I'm not backing down. I will do whatever it takes or say whatever I need to in order to recover my memory and continue my career. It's my true calling, whether you realize it or not."

She had watched his expression fluctuate as she spoke. He was definitely listening.

"My apologies, Ms. Jones," Reed said soberly. "You're right. I was assuming too much." He noted the time. "The dogs have been alone for almost half an hour. I need to go check on them. How long will it take you to pack?"

"Not long." She wanted to keep him in sight, to lean on his strength despite her speech to the contrary. "Why don't you go get them and bring them up here for a few minutes while I grab an overnight bag and fill it?"

"I can do that," Reed replied.

She could tell he was as hesitant to leave as she was to have him go. When he suggested she walk down with him to get the dogs, she was more than happy to oblige. Noting how cautiously he entered the hallway before permitting her to join him helped reinforce her decision to move. Staying on edge day and night was not conducive to her mental healing.

To Abigail's consternation, she was literally yearning to remain near Reed. He'd become her anchor in the maelstrom whirling around her, the only steadying influence in her life.

Everyone else needed *her* to help *them*. Only Reed Branson stood ready to give support instead of taking it.

With Abigail to coax Midnight to try, the gangly pup made it up the stairs. By the third floor the younger dog was gamboling and panting and wagging her tail as if she'd just climbed Mt. Everest.

"She did it!" Abigail acted almost as excited as the ebony pup.

It pleased Reed to see how delighted the two of them were by their shared accomplishment. Let them celebrate while they could. He was still on protection duty. All he had to do was keep Abby from noticing his diligence.

Using the shortened version of her name in his thoughts made him ask aloud, "Does anybody ever call you Abby?"

Her smile disappeared. "My mother used to. I don't care for it, if you don't mind."

"Sorry."

"Don't be. It would have been better for me if Mom had hit the road with Dad when he left."

"Did your mother divorce him? Remarry?"

He held the apartment door for her and they entered with the dogs.

"Nope. But she had plenty of boyfriends."

"Is that why you left?" He could tell she was debating whether or not to explain and he knew he shouldn't have pressed her, so he added, "Never mind. It's none of my business."

"I wasn't going to put it like that. I'd just rather not discuss it." Pink color rose in her cheeks. "Those are memories I wish I could forget the way I've blacked out getting attacked."

"Have you recalled anything about that night?" he asked, glad for a change of subject.

Thoughtful, she passed him Midnight's leash and stepped back. "Just little glimmers. A thought will start to form, then disappear. Like the foggy shadows."

"What shadows?"

"It's hard to explain. I can be thinking of something else and a picture of shadowy figures will flash into my mind. The harder I try to focus on it, the quicker the scene is gone."

"What did it remind you of? People?"

"I think so. More than one. And when we went to my office to meet with Kiera, I got a flash of something that made the hair on my arms stand on end." She shivered. "It was as though I was seeing her as part of the attack."

"Do you think she was?"

Abigail was shaking her head vigorously. "No. I do wonder if one of my other cases might have been involved, though. Those kids stick together. It's possible that Kiera knows more than she's willing to admit."

Reed nodded. "Okay. One thing at a time. I'll wait with the dogs while you go pack. Make it fast. We want to get out of here ASAP."

"Do you think the prowler will come back?"

What should he do? Reed asked himself. Tell her the truth and make her fearful or reassure her when he could be wrong?

"I don't have a clue," he said honestly. "The only thing I am sure of is that you'll be safer someplace else."

Mirroring his nod, she squared her shoulders and stood tall. "Thank you," she said flatly. "I appreciate your candor."

The sight of this slightly built, lovely young woman displaying so much inner strength despite the circumstances took him by surprise. When she'd told him she possessed hidden fortitude, he'd doubted her. Now he was seeing it for himself.

Nothing changed about her either, as she left him and went to pack. Was she really as strong as she acted or was she putting on a front to keep from showing her true feelings?

Her bravery had to be genuine, he reasoned.

When he'd first met her, she had been a basket case, so traumatized she could barely speak let alone function normally. There was no way she could be faking this much recovery. The real Abigail Jones was emerging and it gave him pause. While she'd seemed so broken, he could justify spending an inordinate amount of time looking after her. Now that she was regaining fortitude, she needed him far less.

Reed knew he should be glad she wasn't quite so needy anymore. Part of him was thrilled.

The disquieting element of the change in Abigail was his realization that he was also disappointed.

A last look at her apartment as she locked the door behind her made Abigail feel strangely sad. It wasn't much but it was home. No other place had ever seemed so dear, so safe, so comforting. And now that sense of peace had been stolen from her just as surely as if a thief had stripped the rooms bare.

Reed was waiting in the hall with the dogs. "I see you travel light."

"I don't need much besides my phone and a couple changes of clothes. Once you bring me my purse I'll have everything." She purposely neglected to mention that a large chunk of her salary was spent on others, especially the kids she was trying to coax off the streets. A Fresh Start had a budget for essentials but it barely covered the most basic necessities, and it gave her pleasure to add whatever she could. Although her boss was aware of some of her largesse the directors of the program had no clue about its scope, which was exactly how she wanted it.

"We'll go first," Reed said, gesturing at the stairwell. "Stick close."

"Hey, if you were wearing a backpack I'd climb into it," Abigail told him with a nervous chuckle.

"If we didn't have the puppy with us I could put Jessie at heel and carry you the way I did at Luna Park."

Hearing that caused her pulse to jump. "You what?"

"Carried you." He glanced over his shoulder. "Sorry. I shouldn't talk about that night because I don't want to influence your memories. The mind is a funny thing. People tend to fill in details they don't know, without realizing it, because their brain isn't satisfied with loose ends."

"Really?"

"Yes. Really."

Sticking close to his back, she almost ran into him when he stopped at the outer door to check the busy sidewalk and street beyond.

Abigail had to smile. "My neighbors will be glad to see me go. Anything to keep you from blocking traffic so often."

"It was necessary."

"I know. And I thank you. Again. I just hate to see so many drivers upset with the police."

"Yeah. Until they need us themselves. Then it's different." Reed shrugged. "Come on. Let's get your stuff and these dogs stowed and get out of here."

She followed closely, trying to help yet also stay out of his way. In seconds they were back on the road.

"Tell me about your sister," Abigail said.

That brought a smile. "Lani's amazing. She's been a dancer and an actress and also taught self-defense."

"I thought she was a cop, like you?"

"She is." Reed's smile spread. "The last time she reinvented herself, she decided she wanted to follow in my footsteps and work with K-9s. I didn't try to talk her out of it because I never dreamed she'd get this far. She surprised me and by not only getting into K-9 training but managing to transfer to my unit when she graduated."

"I'd have thought siblings wouldn't be allowed."

He laughed. "Normally, they aren't. My unit is unique, and Lani made the most of it."

"I hope she likes me."

"Lani likes everybody. She can be a bit over-whelming if you're not used to her personality. Just go with the flow."

With a silent sigh Abigail leaned back in the seat and folded her hands in her lap. Isolation and quiet was what she loved about the apartment she'd just left. Chaos often haunted her at work and she looked forward to calm, solitary evenings reading a good book or maybe watching an old movie on TV. Moving in with Reed and his sister, plus the dogs was likely to make going to her job seem like a sanctuary instead of the other way around.

Well, it couldn't be helped. She'd cope. Some-how. After all, the change was only temporary. Her apartment would be there when she was ready to go home.

A catch in her throat brought unshed tears to her eyes and she coughed to cover the reac-tion. When she had thought of home just now, she had realized that her feelings had been al-tered by the presence of the prowler. He might not have taken concrete objects from her, but he had stolen just the same. He had robbed her of what little peace she'd had left and there wasn't a thing she could do about it.

Casting a sidelong glance at Reed, she won-dered how long his altruism was going to last.

What if his sister pitched a fit at him for bringing home a houseguest and she had to find other accommodations? Where would she go? She could barely afford one place to live. Paying for a second one while trying to break her lease in Brighton Beach was out of the question.

Abigail turned to stare out the side window, barely heeding the passing cityscape. Her heart and mind turned to the only true anchor she had, her wavering yet tenacious faith. Sensible prayer was difficult when she was so confused, so adrift.

Out of her scarred memory came a Bible truth. *God takes care of the flowers of the fields and the birds of the air, so consider how much better He will provide for his children.*

It didn't spell out the path she must follow, but it did speak of trusting the Lord. Given her current circumstances, Abigail figured that was the best advice around.

All she had to do was make it happen.

Easier said than done.

Faith was not a tangible thing that could be grabbed and stuffed into a box for safekeeping. It was a state of mind, an acceptance of God's invisible power and unqualified acceptance, no matter what a person had or hadn't done. That was why turning your life over to Christ was sometimes so difficult.

And yet, over time, Abigail had experienced the Lord's kindness, His leading, His unending presence in the midst of her worst trials. Looking back, it was easy to see how He had protected her in the past and had guided her steps into the present. Setting aside her misgivings, she knew without a doubt that she was blessed.

Her gaze drifted to the driver on her left. A week ago they didn't even know each other, and today she was on her way to live in his house. Either that was divine guidance or she was about to dive into worse trouble than she'd ever imagined.

Hopefully it was the former and would turn out to be another blessing. That was certainly her unspoken prayer.

TEN

Reed's residential street in Queens was different from hers in Brighton Beach. For one thing, it was quieter. He slowed, waved at a group of neighbor kids shooting hoops in a driveway, then pulled to the curb across the street. "This is it."

"Wow. Parking practically in front of the house!"

He laughed. "Living out here has its perks. I would have stopped in the driveway if I thought our upstairs tenant was home. He gets the garage. I park outside. Having a police car out front is a great crime deterrent."

"I would think so."

Glad to see her spirits rising, Reed wisely avoided mentioning the mood change. Instead, he climbed out, leashed the dogs and released them. The pup was so excited she was running circles around Jessie and twisting together their light leashes.

Abigail retrieved her overnight bag and joined him. "Looks like they're glad to be here."

"Yeah. Me, too." He gestured at the white, two-story dwelling on its narrow lot. Houses on either side were clearly the same floor plan but had been modified over time by their various owners. The Branson place had a stone facade with short pillars next to the sidewalk to denote the beginning of the entry path. What lawn there was had been mowed recently, and flower beds graced a narrow strip fronting the porch.

"It's pretty," Abigail said. "Very welcoming."

"You can thank Lani," he replied. "She's the one who plants the flowers. I will admit I did some of the painting but only because she made me."

"*Made* you? I doubt that."

"Okay, she guilted me into helping her." He knew there was a goofy grin on his face but for some reason it felt right.

"That, I can believe."

As Reed shepherded his little group up the steps and onto the porch, he experienced an unanticipated surge of emotion. Lacking a different definition, he named it *joy*. Really? In the midst of all the conflicts in his work and home life, he was actually joyful? That seemed wrong, particularly in view of the mourning his unit was doing over their late chief, Jordan Jameson. Plus, they were all worried about Katie, Jordy's widow. Katie had been newly pregnant when Jordan was murdered six months ago and not only was she going to have to raise the child alone, she was still in limbo about the identity of her husband's murderer. They all were. So what right did anyone have to be this happy?

Reed had to smile at his twisted thoughts. Jordan Jameson had been a Christian. He'd see his family again someday. It was finding clues to his killer or killers that should be foremost on everybody's mind. Just when they thought they were getting closer to resolving the puzzle, something happened to pull them back. Crime never took a vacation. Drugs, gangs, muggings, drive-by shootings and myriad other events kept the entire police force engaged 24/7.

Opening the door for Abigail, he held back the dogs and paused to give his and Jessie's jobs serious thought. He couldn't help but be thankful that they were tasked with tracking instead of, say, bomb detection. Reed wasn't keen on working with a K-9 whose nose was trained to seek out destruction. His Jessie found lost people and that was fine with him.

Case in point. His gaze fastened on Abigail as she perused the small living room. If he hadn't been assigned to look for Snapper on the boardwalk at exactly the right time, not only might he have failed to meet her, she might have received more serious injuries. That thought deposited a boulder in the pit of his stomach. Thank God that he was around when she'd needed him.

"This is lovely," Abigail said. "You and your sister share the downstairs?"

"Yes. And the kitchen. Lani keeps telling me that cooking isn't necessarily a woman's job so we take turns."

"In other words, you order out?" Abigail was smiling at him and his cheeks warmed.

"Sometimes. I make a mean hamburger when I can grill in the backyard."

"How often have you done it with snow on the ground?" she asked.

Reed had to laugh. "A few. How did you know?"

"I'm a good guesser."

Reed passed her, leading both dogs. "I'll go let these girls out the back door and then show you your room. When I phoned Lani she said she'd move and give you her room but I figured you'd turn it down. The same goes for mine."

"You know me pretty well."

"I like to think so."

Just then the front door burst open, startling everyone. A young blonde woman wearing workout clothes that accented her athleticism was making her usual theatrical entrance. "Hi!

You must be Abigail." She dropped overfull totes on the floor and stuck out her right hand. "I'm Lani, Reed's sister. Welcome to Queens. I picked up a few groceries. We'll order a pizza for supper. You like pizza, don't you? Of course you do. Everybody loves a good New York pizza."

Abigail briefly shook hands. "Hello."

"Has Reed shown you your room? I told him you could have my bed but he was sure you wouldn't accept it so I made up a cot in the spare room. It's usually an office. I hope you don't mind. I know it's not much but it's all we have."

Watching Abigail's reaction to Lani's monologue brought a grin and almost made Reed laugh out loud. His sister was a whirlwind of enthusiasm no matter what she was doing. Today was no exception. If Abigail ever managed to get a word in edgeways he was certain they would find common ground and get along well.

He held up a hand. "Whoa. Calm down, sis. We just got here a minute ago. I haven't even had time to put the dogs out."

Lani returned his smile and shrugged. "Sorry. I just want our guest to feel at home."

"I'm sure I will," Abigail said. "Right now, everything is kind of overwhelming." She met Lani's gaze. "Did Reed tell you about my loss of memory?"

"He mentioned it, yes." Lani took Abigail's

hand and patted it. "We'll get you back to normal soon, I promise. He said you were attacked. I used to teach self-defense, you know. While you're here I can give you lessons."

The black puppy was tugging at the leash and trying to chew it. Reed ignored her long enough to counter his sister's suggestion. "I don't think that's such a great idea, Lani. Abigail will be plenty safe staying with us. She doesn't need instructions in hand-to-hand fighting. She's far better off relying on the police."

By the time he finished making his point, both women were staring at him. Lani was making a silly face and Abigail looked irate. That was not good. He figured he was about to learn plenty about her opinion. When she fisted her hands on her hips he was positive.

"You're joking, right?"

What could he tell her except the truth? "Um, no."

She rolled her eyes at him, then at Lani. "Do you believe this guy?"

"Sure," Lani said with a chuckle. "He's my brother. He's always underestimating me."

"Me, too." Abigail began to smile. "I'll be ready for my first self-defense lesson when you are. In the meantime I'll help you carry the groceries to the kitchen."

"My kind of houseguest," Lani said with enthusiasm. "C'mon, Abby. Grab a bag."

"She doesn't like that nickname," Reed called after them. A lot of good it did him. They disappeared into the kitchen together as if they had rehearsed a stage exit from one of Lani's little theater productions.

"Humph." Reed looked down at the dogs. Jessie was waiting for a command while Midnight nibbled on the bloodhound's ear. "I'm surrounded," he quipped. "Outnumbered by females." Starting for the back door he said, "All right, girls. Let's go outside and get some air. I need a break as much as you do."

Boy, was that the truth! When he'd suggested that Abigail meet and share a home with him and Lani, he hadn't imagined a joining of forces. It wouldn't hurt Lani to absorb a little of Abigail's sweet nature, but he sure hoped the influence didn't flow both ways. If it did, he was going to have more trouble than ever convincing Abigail to take his advice.

It struck Abigail funny that she had taken to both Branson siblings so easily. They were not terribly alike, yet each had a way of making her feel welcome. While Lani called to order a pizza, she busied herself pulling fresh vegetables out of the totes and lining them up on the counter.

"This romaine looks fantastic," Abigail remarked. "There's a greengrocer's close to my place in Brighton Beach. I shop there often." *When I'm not hiding from my own shadow.*

"Fresh is always the best. I have to walk a couple blocks farther but it's worth it." Lani paused. "Reed tells me you've had it pretty rough lately. I hope staying with us gives you a break. I can't imagine being by myself all the time."

Puzzled, Abigail tilted her head to one side. "Really? Why should you be worried when you're a cop and you know self-defense?"

Lani smiled sweetly. "I'm not afraid. I just know I'd be lonesome, even once I get my K-9 assignment. I like people around me." She giggled. "Even my stuffy brother."

"Stuffy? I never noticed that about Reed. He's always seemed very helpful and upbeat."

"Yeah? Pass me the salad makings," Lani said, opening a crisper drawer in the refrigerator. While she was bent over, putting the produce away, she said, "Personally, I think Reed is a great guy, too. Trouble is, he eats, sleeps and breathes the K-9 unit. That doesn't leave time for a social life."

Abigail was fairly certain Lani was issuing an unnecessary warning, so she countered with her own explanation. "I'm sure there is nothing *social* about your brother's concern for my welfare. He was the officer who first found me after I was attacked and has kindly shepherded me through the beginning of my healing process. It's not personal."

"If you say so. He seems to like you a lot, though. I'd hate to see him hurt."

The notion of her self-appointed protector being hurt, physically or emotionally, slammed into Abigail like a rogue Atlantic wave. All this time, while Reed had been looking after her welfare, she hadn't properly considered his. Well, she would now. The immensity of his sacrifice was just beginning to register. Before, she had let herself fall into the trap of feeling helpless and hopeless because of her lapse of memory. From now on she intended to be proactive.

How she was going to accomplish that remained as unknown as her insight into the attack at the park or the traffic accident or the break-in at her apartment. Although she already had all the human assistance she needed, she realized she had failed to pray for continuing guidance and wisdom. Doing so properly, however, was best accomplished in private, so she asked, "Would you mind if I went to my room to freshen up a bit before supper?"

"Not at all. Where are my manners? Hang on a sec and I'll show you to your room."

"I can take her," Reed offered, stepping in the back door without the dogs. "The furry contingent is playing on the grass."

"Okay, if you don't mind." For some reason Abigail found herself feeling shy.

"Not a bit." He picked up her suitcase and gestured with his free arm like a courtier in a medieval drama. "After you."

Abigail had not forgotten why she sought solitude, although if anything could have distracted her it was the handsome K-9 cop. They proceeded down a short hallway, stopping at the end. One look confirmed that the room Lani had prepared for her had been a home office. That didn't matter. It had a door and blinds on the windows. That was all the privacy she needed

She paused in the doorway, blocking it and facing Reed. "Thank you. For everything."

He handed her the suitcase. "If you need anything, just ask. Lani says supper will be in about an hour, but if you want to rest longer, that's no problem."

"An hour will be fine," Abigail said. The small room behind her beckoned as if it wanted her to feel at home. She started to close the door.

Reed backed up. "Okay, then."

Truth to tell, Abigail didn't want to close him

out, but she needed privacy in order to bare her soul to her heavenly Father. There was so much that she didn't understand, so many loose ends to the events of recent days, she felt as if she were far beyond her depth and being pulled under by an unseen riptide.

The latch clicked into place. Abigail pressed her back to the closed door and sighed noisily. Her thoughts reached out to God while her body was hit with intense fatigue. She was spent in more ways than mere physical exertion. Her heart was bruised by the way Kiera had treated her, her thoughts were murky and disconnected, and she was almost as bereft as she had been the day she'd decided to run away to escape the unhealthy life her mother had chosen.

After making her way to the narrow bed, she perched on the edge, bowed her head, closed her eyes, folded her hands and whispered, "Oh, Father, I'm so lost. I don't know how I got here or what's next. Please, please show me. Help me?"

In her mind she could almost hear, *Peace, be still.* Wishful thinking sometimes manifested that way when she was overwrought. And yet, there was a certain almost tangible peace flowing over and around her as if she were being wrapped in a cloud of warmth and security.

Abigail resisted the sensation. She didn't want to be cosseted, she wanted to be useful, in charge, making a difference the way she did in the lives of the teenage runaways who came into her office. She wanted to know what had happened to her and take an active role in bringing her attackers to justice. She wanted...

Truth struck her hard. She wanted to tell the Lord how to run her little universe. Of all the errors she'd made lately, that was undoubtedly the worst, the most foolish.

Turning her thoughts, her deepest heart, back to prayer, she began with an apology. "Forgive me, Jesus. Forgive me. Please. I know you only want what's best for me." Abigail inhaled a shuddery breath and let it out slowly. As long as she relied upon her faith, she didn't need to know the details of God's ultimate plan.

Trusting Him was the key. It always had been, even when she'd been adrift and living on the streets like the kids she helped. That was when she had come to a spiritual awakening, thanks to several mentors. It had been as if the Lord had lined those believers up in His divine order and introduced them into her life at the exact moment when she was ready to accept the teaching each offered.

Grateful beyond words, Abigail realized that she still could have rejected the faith that now buoyed her up through this tempest. "Thank you, Father," she said, barely whispering as tears of thankfulness trickled down her cheeks.

Eyes closed, she continued in wordless gratitude, heart and mind. Each day demanded renewed commitment to her heavenly Father, just as each night required that she put her trust in His perfect wisdom and mercy.

Night. Shadows. A memory wafted through her mind like windblown smoke.

Abigail tensed. Almost lost touch with the vision. There were three figures, two tall and one much shorter. The little one stood between the other two and was struggling.

Her eyes popped open. Reality immediately intruded, yet she managed to retain the elusive insight.

Jumping to her feet, she swiped away her tears, hurried to the door and jerked it open to yell, "Reed!"

ELEVEN

Hearing Abigail shout his name sent Reed's heart into orbit. They nearly knocked each other down when they collided in the hallway.

He grasped her shoulders and set her away so he could look into her face. "What's wrong?"

"Nothing." She was beaming through a mist of tears. "I remembered something. It was as clear as if I were looking right at it."

Struggling to control his pounding pulse, he slipped an arm around her shoulders and guided her toward the living room sofa. "Okay. Have a seat and tell me."

She twisted away, clearly elated. "No! I can't sit still. Listen. There were two guys at Luna Park that night. And a smaller person, probably a girl or young man. One guy was hanging onto the littler person and she—or he—was struggling to escape. I saw it all. I remember now."

He wasn't about to spoil her moment of triumph by mentioning that he'd likely observed the same two adults. Hearing that there had been a younger person involved was a definite break-through.

"Go on," Reed urged, working to keep his voice even and his tone casual. "What did you do then?"

Abigail deflated like a Mylar balloon on its third day. "I don't know. I didn't remember that far."

"It's okay," he was quick to tell her. "These things take time. You've made excellent prog-ress. I have no doubt the rest of your memories will return soon."

"I should have tried to hold on to the vision."

"Not necessarily. You said you'd done that before with poor results. What you got, you got clearly. That's a big plus. We didn't know about the younger person before just now."

Abigail perked up a little and grasped his forearm. "Do you think it could have been Kiera they were holding? Is that why she was so eva-sive?"

"That's one possibility. Another is that she's the reason you were out there that night. Maybe you were going to meet her, she saw what was happening and split instead of trying to help. You told me she was obviously lying about why she wanted to talk to you at the center. She may have been embarrassed to admit deserting you the other night and wanted to know if you were aware she'd been nearby."

"You could be right." Sighing, Abigail looked to Lani, who had frozen in place to listen while holding a bowl of tossed salad. "What do you think?"

"Me? I'm just a rookie, but if this girl Kiera was acting funny after that night, I'd be inclined to peg her as a witness. Most victims put off different vibes. Did she seem afraid?"

"Not as afraid as I still felt," Abigail replied. "Just leaving my apartment was a major challenge." She shivered.

Reed slipped his arm around her shoulders without stopping to think first. His instinct for protection insisted, overruling any sense of propriety. Although his sister arched an eyebrow quizzically, he didn't back down. The flashes of normalcy they were seeing from Abigail were promising, yes, but that didn't mean she was cured. Until she could willingly recall the entire incident at the carousel, she wasn't out of the woods. Figuratively or literally.

He guided her to the kitchen table, essentially turning her over to his sister. "I'm going to make a quick call to headquarters and notify the 60th Precinct, too. They need to be aware that there was a teenage victim involved in the first assault on Ms. Jones."

Lani was quick to reply. "Gotcha. If you're going outside to call it in, watch for the pizza man."

Nodding, Reed pulled out his cell and headed for the front door. Once he was outside he contacted his dispatcher and relayed Abigail's information, completing the call just as a pickup stopped at the curb. A man balancing a full pizza warmer jumped out and started up the walk.

Reed waved. "What do I owe you?"

He paid, took the hot pie and turned toward the open door, calling, "Thanks!" over his shoulder.

"No problem, man," the harried driver shouted back.

Reed had time to take only one step before he heard Abigail shriek.

She clapped both hands over her mouth. That voice. Did it belong to one of her attackers? At first hearing she'd thought so, but now that several seconds had passed she was growing less and less certain. Had the recent glimpse of lost memory triggered an aberration in her reasoning processes? Rather than remembering his voice, had she merely imagined a similarity?

Reed thrust the box at his sister and cupped Abigail's shoulders. "What happened? You're shaking."

"I thought… I thought…"

"You thought what?"

"That man's voice. It reminded me of someone. He couldn't have been the guy from the boardwalk, could he?"

"Of course he could."

"Did you know him? I mean, is he your regular delivery guy?"

"One of them," Reed told her. "Look, just because he sounded like the man who accosted you doesn't mean he's the same one, but there's nothing to prove he isn't until we check his alibi for the night you were chased." He guided her to the sofa. "Sit here while I make a couple more calls."

Abigail hated to keep following his orders but at the moment, sitting down seemed quite sensible. So did listening to his phone conversation. There was no doubt he was talking to the police, either his own unit or the one responsible for that Queens neighborhood.

"That's right," Reed said. "The pizza delivery was just made to my house. I want a check on the driver and his alibi for every night last week. If he was working, I want to know where his route took him." He listened for a brief minute, then added, "There's a chance he may tie to the Luna Park incident I worked when we were down there looking for Jordan Jameson's dog, Snapper."

Watching his expression, Abigail saw him listen and begin to frown.

"When? Where? Okay, stand by." Reed cupped a palm over the receiver and spoke aside to her. "What do you know about a kid named Dominic Walenski?"

Her breath caught and she swallowed a gasp. "Why?"

"So, you do know him?"

"Yes. What's going on?"

"An anonymous caller reported that he's been kidnapped. When I mentioned Luna Park they told me that's where he was last seen."

"Oh, no!" Abigail managed to pull herself together enough to provide background. "Dom looks a lot younger than Kiera but he's almost her age. They're both part of a group that hangs out on the boardwalk most of the time."

"Okay." Listening to the phone, Reed held up his index finger to signal silence, so she waited. It wasn't easy. Dom was as much one of her kids as Kiera, maybe more so, considering the off-putting way that girl had been behaving lately. Abigail spread trembling hands wide, palms up, and mouthed, *Well?*

"All right," Reed said into the phone. "Jessie and I will stand by." He ended the call.

"What else did they say?"

"Not much. Apparently the tip came from an anonymous source. Female. Refused to give her name."

"We need to go. *I* need to go," Abigail insisted.

"In due time. Let the beat cops sort it out before we blunder in and cause more confusion. They're on scene. If they decide there's anything to the report, Jessie and I will be dispatched."

Lani interrupted, a pizza-laden plate in each hand. "You'd better eat, then. No telling how long you'll be gone if you get the call."

"Not both of us," Reed insisted, accepting the generous slices. "Abigail is staying here with you."

"Oh yeah?" Abigail was adamant. "Even if Jessie manages to track some of the kids down they'll take one look at you and scatter. You may not like it, but you need me."

"Aren't you scared?"

She huffed. "Of course I am! I'm terrified. Who wouldn't be? But that's no excuse for abandoning one of my kids when he's in danger."

"*If* he is."

Expecting further argument, she was stunned when Reed thrust the second plate toward her and said, "Then eat. And use a fork so you don't get Italian spices on your hands and confuse my dog."

She was going? Reed was including her? Just like that?

Averting her face to hide a flash of victory, she took a place at the kitchen table. Lani provided cutlery and a cold soda over ice.

Well, well, well, Abigail thought. *Just when I think I have him figured out, he goes and surprises me. What's up with that?*

A bigger question involved motive. Was Reed taking her along because he thought he would need her, as she'd claimed, or was he simply hoping that a return to the Coney Island boardwalk would further jog her memory? Either was possible. It didn't matter. As long as she continued to put others first and strive to do the job she was positive had been divinely ordained, she'd be fine.

Peeking over at him through lowered lashes, she realized she was ready and willing to follow him just about anywhere on earth. That admission was terribly unsettling. And patently true.

The dispatch for Jessie and Reed came a half hour after the initial report. He was in uniform by then. Jessie took one look at her official K-9 vest and harness and began quivering with excitement.

Reed eyed Abigail. She, too, was trembling, though not from eagerness, he concluded. *I have to hand it to her. That woman's got courage.*

"Ready?" He was strapping on his gear and checking the extra search and rescue equipment clipped to his vest and tucked into a go-bag.

Abigail's fingers were laced together at her waist and the knuckles had begun whitening. "I'm ready when you are."

"Okay. Come on. We'll go over procedure in the car."

He felt her following closely as he strode to the blue-and-white SUV. While he loaded Jessie, Abigail climbed into the passenger seat and was fumbling with her safety belt as he slid behind the wheel, grabbed the radio and reported his status.

"Branson leaving Queens. Do you want a code three response?"

"Negative," the dispatcher broadcast. "Units on scene report that the claims are so far unsubstantiated. Just keep your eyes open."

"What about a scent package?"

"Reporting party is supposed to meet you at the corner of West Fifteenth and Surf Avenue. She says she will have an article of clothing."

"Copy." Reed cleared his throat. "I have an

outreach worker ride-along. She knows the Walenski boy personally."

"You cleared that with Noah?" was loud and clear.

Reed clenched his jaw. "Chief Jameson is aware I've been assisting this person in my off-duty time." He wanted to add that Abigail was up to her pretty blue eyeballs in this hot mess, but refrained. The less said, the better. He'd ask for forgiveness later rather than delay long enough to obtain official permission to include her.

"Copy," the dispatcher said.

He glanced across the front seat at his scowling passenger. "You knew I wasn't keeping track of you on the department's dime, didn't you?"

"I'd guessed as much." Her slim fingers had returned to their interwoven position.

"Just remember that this time is going to be different," Reed warned. "When Jessie and I are working you have to stay well behind us so you don't disturb any scent she picks up. Even a slight breeze can be too much. Got that?"

"Yes, sir. So how am I supposed to help you find Dominic if I'm trailing behind you?"

"Hopefully, whoever gives us the scented article of clothing will be connected to the group he normally runs with. You'll introduce me and vouch for me then."

"But…"

The quaver in her voice told him more than words would have. She was every bit as scared as he'd assumed she'd be even though she was putting on a brave front. How long she could maintain that facade was what concerned him.

"I won't be walking slowly after Jessie strikes a trail. Keep up with us as best you can. Run if you have to. Once my K-9 is committed I won't stop and wait for you. Understood?"

Abigail was nodding, her gaze wide. "Got it. What if I lose sight of you?"

"Then find the nearest patrol officer and stick to him or her. We'll return eventually, with or without the Walenski kid."

He had anticipated an argument he didn't get. The rest of the drive to Coney Island was uneventful until they approached the rendezvous point and noted the crowd.

Abigail leaned forward and pointed at a gaggle of teens amassed on the street corner. "That's them! Kiera's posse. There she is. Standing by the front patrol car. See?"

Reed saw all right. And what he saw was disquieting. If the entire group was worried enough to willingly meet and mingle with the police, chances were good that Dominic actually had been abducted as the caller had insisted.

He could tell these kids sure thought Dominic Walenski was in trouble. And since *they* did, that was good enough for him.

TWELVE

Abigail clicked off her seat belt and yanked the handle of the door before Reed had come to a complete stop. He checked in with the officers on scene while Abigail scanned the milling throng. Rides and concession stands were still open and the place was packed with New Yorkers and tourists eager to get in a last hurrah before the season ended.

Kiera ran forward waving a blue satin windbreaker. "I have Dom's jacket," the teen told Abigail. "He never leaves it. Never. His mom gave it to him right before…before she left."

"All right. That's good." Abigail gestured toward the approaching K-9 officer. "Kiera, this is Officer Branson and his bloodhound, Jessie. She's a tracker. Give the jacket to him and let him get to work."

The girl complied, eyeing Reed and Abigail suspiciously. "If you say so but I'm going too. We all are."

Hearing her own demand echoing back at her and realizing how off base she, too, had been, Abigail stopped. "We will. But in order for Jessie to work we all have to hang behind. Otherwisc wc can confuse her. Okay?" She slipped an arm around Kiera's shoulders to lightly restrain her. "The best way to find Dom is to follow the rules, even if we don't like them." A sidelong glance at Reed showed her his raised eyebrows. If the situation had not been so serious she might have smiled at the irony.

"I'll stay behind with these guys," Abigail told him, seeing his satisfaction with her choice.

He stepped forward, jacket in hand, and addressed the crowd. "Who was the last one to see Dominic?"

A dozen hands shot up.

Reed rephrased, eyeing a nearby patrolman. "You talked to that officer, right? Did he work out a timeline?"

Kiera pressed forward. "Yeah. It was me. Dom was supposed to meet us at our special place." She blushed. "We like to sit on a fave bench, eat hot dogs and watch the sunset."

"It's not dark yet. What makes you so sure something bad has happened to him?" Reed asked.

Abigail noted the way he was scanning the youthful faces and did the same. A couple of the boys were looking away as if they were hiding something, so she left Kiera and worked her way to them.

Keeping her body language relaxed, she slipped an arm around the slim shoulders of each boy and leaned in closer. "Okay, guys. Give. What do you know about all this?"

The taller of the two twisted away and ducked into the crowd of curious onlookers. The younger child was trapped, quivering. She kept a tight hold. "This police officer is my friend," she said. "He just wants to help us. Tell me whatever you know about Dom."

"He—he said he was gonna score. Be rich."

Abigail's thoughts immediately went to crime. "Drugs?"

"No! He'd never do that."

"Then what? What was he up to?"

"I don't know. Honest."

"Did you actually see him taken?" Reed asked.

The teen shook his head.

"Okay," Abigail announced. "Everybody listen up. Kiera is going to show Officer Branson where she saw Dominic last and then we'll back off so his dog can sniff and follow the scent. All of us. Got that?"

There were enough muttered assents to allay her fears that the kids would stampede through

Jessie's scent trail. Grasping Kiera's shoulders, she turned her toward Reed and gestured to him. "Lead on."

Accompanying the teen, Reed guided Jessie toward the boardwalk. They weren't far from where he'd come upon Abigail that first time and he wondered what was going through her mind. Hopefully, having all those familiar young people clustering around her would be good for her taut nerves. And her lost memory. This was not the method he would have chosen to minister to her, but who was he to argue with God? After all, if he believed divine providence had led him to Abigail before, he almost had to credit the same source this time.

That was the trouble with faith, Reed mused. Sometimes it was easy to imagine the Lord's beneficial influence in a person's life while other times the choices seemed so impossible. It often boiled down to total acceptance or none. Too bad that degree of commitment wasn't as simple as it sounded.

Walking ahead, Kiera stopped just short of the boardwalk and waited for him. Yellow crime scene tape was draped across one side of the path while several patrol officers directed regular beachgoers out and around the cordoned-off area.

"Like I told the other cops, we were right here," she said. "Dominic promised to be back in ten minutes. It's been almost a whole day." Her voice broke.

Reed stopped short. "You reported that he was kidnapped so that we'd respond right away," he said. "Why? What's the rest of the story?"

She dropped her gaze to her sandals, suddenly fascinated with her toes. "I didn't say…" Her words faded.

"Speak up."

"I didn't say he was kidnapped," she admitted, making a face. "Not exactly."

"But you did mention it?"

The girl shook her head, pink-streaked hair fluttering. "Maybe. I just wanted you guys to find him, okay?"

"Making a false police report is a crime," Reed said gruffly. "We can't afford to run all over the city for no reason."

"I had a reason."

"So, nobody saw him actually being abducted?"

"Uh-uh. I just had a really bad feeling when he didn't come back. He always comes back when he says he will. Always." Kiera brightened and met his gaze. "Maybe he left to look for the dog again."

Reed tensed. "Dog? What dog?"

"The one he got when he was in foster care. Those parents said he couldn't keep it so he ran away and ended up here, with us. Dom said a man gave him that dog and told him it was okay, but the dog won't stay. He runs away a lot."

"Why would he worry about one stray dog? New York is full of them."

"Not like this one." Kiera began to sound enthusiastic. "He was like a super dog, you know? Big and smart and all. Dom said we should keep him for protection but he wouldn't eat good. I mean, we got hot dogs and nachos and stuff out of the trash, like always. He'd just look at the food like there was something wrong with it unless he dug it out himself—or Dom put it in a real dish for him."

Reed's pulse leaped into overdrive. His voice rose. "Was the dog a German shepherd? Was he wearing a collar?"

"Yeah. He had a metal name tag thingy fastened to it, too."

"Snapper," Reed breathed.

Kiera startled. "How did you know?"

"Because he's one of our specially trained K-9s. He's been missing since spring." He presented the jacket to Jessie and encouraged her to sniff it thoroughly as he spoke to the girl. "You go back and find Ms. Jones."

"Why?"

"Because I said so." Reed was nearly shouting. "Tell her what you just told me about Dom, then stay with the others. Those officers will be the first to know when my K-9 tracks down your friend."

And, God willing, Jordan Jameson's canine partner, Reed added to himself. He was beginning to see where this was going and the possibility of solving Jordy's murder loomed large. Finding Snapper, locating the missing boy and getting a lead on a ruthless killer all at once might seem impossible to most people, but it didn't to Reed. Not now.

Kiera dashed at the tears streaking her cheeks as she rejoined Abigail. "I'm sorry. Okay? I didn't mean to make the cops mad."

"Mad? What makes you think anyone's mad at you?"

"Your cop buddy was yelling."

Abigail folded her arms across her chest and stood firm. "Then you must have said something to set him off. I've seen Officer Branson in action and he's not short-tempered. He's always acted polite and professional, even when he's not on duty."

The fact that the teen had averted her gaze and was fidgeting told Abigail she was on the right track. "Tell me exactly what he said to you."

"I don't remember."

"Yes, you do. Give."

"He was mad 'cause I lied so they'd come look for Dom, okay?" Her voice was shrill, reedy. "I knew they wouldn't care if one of us kids was lost or in trouble. Not unless I told them a good story. So I said he was kidnapped." She sniffled. "I don't know why your cop friend had to make a federal case out of it. I mean, it was just a little fib."

Sighing and shaking her head, Abigail got the picture. Many teens didn't consider the consequences of an act before carrying it out. Their brains weren't fully developed yet and although they might look mature and try to behave like adults, their inherent immaturity regularly shot them down.

"Suppose someone else needed Officer Branson and his K-9 while he was here at the beach? What if a little kid got lost or something? Or suppose a murderer escaped because that tracking dog was too busy to chase him?"

"They've got a million dogs. I see 'em all the time."

"Not quite that many. That's not the point. Not all police dogs do the same jobs."

"How do you know?"

"I looked it up." Abigail gently touched the girl's thin shoulder. "Look, honey. I know your heart was in the right place. You guys feel responsible for each other. I think of all of you as family, too. But I'd never make a false police report. That sets a terrible precedent. What do you suppose will happen if you need to call for help again? Will they believe you? Huh?"

"I dunno."

"Well, I do. Come on. We'll start with the officers that came in patrol cars and then ask permission for you to speak to dispatch."

"What for?" The teen hesitated.

Losing patience, Abigail grasped her wrist. "So you can apologize."

"No way. Uh-uh. Not happening. Kids get snatched all the time down here and nobody cares. Nobody reports them missing. What's to say that Dom didn't really get kidnapped?"

Abigail froze. Kidnapped. *At the beach by the boardwalk. The smaller figure struggling between the two shadowy thugs. Was that what I saw?*

Wide-eyed, she stared at the girl beside her. Could Kiera have witnessed that same event? Was that why she'd sought Abigail out, had been so interested in what she might be able to recall?

Kiera cringed under the scrutiny. "Hey, why are you looking at me like that? It's creepy."

"You were there," Abigail said, hoping a

forceful tone would carry her through. "You saw me get attacked."

Crimson infused Kiera's pale cheeks and clashed with the pink in her hair. "No way."

"Yes way," Abigail insisted. "That's why you insisted on meeting with me face-to-face. Somebody must have told you my memory was bad. You wanted to see if I remembered why I'd gone out that night and what I'd seen before I was attacked. Why, Kiera? Who are you protecting?"

"No-nobody." Twisting, she tried to free her wrist. "Let me go. That hurts!"

Realizing she had inadvertently restrained the teen, Abigail backed off, hands open and raised. "Sorry. Sorry, I wasn't thinking." Unshed tears of frustration filled her eyes. "Please. If you know anything about what happened to me, or to anyone else, you need to tell the police. At least give them a chance. Give me a chance."

"Snitch?" Rubbing her wrist, the wary teen gave a snort of derision. "No way, lady. You can keep your sodas and your food vouchers and your stupid clothes. We'll do okay without any help."

There was nothing more Abigail could say. One moment's lapse in judgment had probably undone most of the good she'd managed to accomplish all summer. Honesty had cost her the trust of this teen and probably would affect many more by the time Kiera finished retelling the tale and giving it her own slant.

At that moment, Abigail yearned to rejoin Reed, to tell him her suspicions and ask his advice on what to do next. Looking past Kiera, she scanned the nearly deserted beach. The tide was coming in. A cadre of police officers were sweeping the shoreline with flashlights, following the path Jessie had taken before the waves rose and washed away all traces.

Abigail shivered. Folded her arms across her chest and hugged herself. One mistake. One little mistake. What had gotten into her? She wasn't a violent person, yet the grip of her fingers on the teen's thin wrist had left a temporary red mark.

She began to mindlessly chafe her own wrist. Sense the unwelcome touch of rough, masculine fingers. She closed her eyes and let the vision develop. Her pulse began to pound in her temples, her breathing the exhausted rasp of weakening prey.

Abigail could smell the sea and the concessions as usual, but beyond that was an odor of filth and sweat and unnamed revulsion. Her gorge rose. The remembered shadows took tenuous shape with noses and squinty eyes and ugly, ugly grins.

She gasped. Her eyes snapped open. The

image vanished. But she had seen more this time. Much more. Those men had grabbed her, held her arms, kept her prisoner. Her fractured memory was healing. Returning. Piece by piece.

Inside the fences of Luna Park stood the antique carousel where Reed had found her cowering. She stared at it, hoping for more details. Trepidation now mingled with elation. Unnamed fear was being displaced by the joy of anticipated relief.

That segment of her escape might still be a mystery, but she was positive it wouldn't remain one for much longer.

THIRTEEN

Jessie led Reed down the shore toward Brighton Beach, then doubled back until they were nearly to the spot where he'd left Abigail and the others. To his right, a line of uniformed officers, augmented by official cleanup crew members in their neon vests, held onlookers at bay.

To his surprise, Jessie paused, sniffed the air, then plowed straight into the gaggle of teens.

Reed noted Abigail standing prominently at the edge of the group. Where was Kiera? Had his impromptu lecture helped the teenager understand the seriousness of falsifying her crime report? He sincerely hoped so.

Instead of stopping to greet Abigail or anybody else, the trusty bloodhound kept her nose to the ground and shouldered through the human barricade at knee level. Jessie was clearly tracking. As long as she was on the trail he wasn't about to pull her back.

The clever K-9 circled a hotdog cart, ducked

behind the vendor's portable sign and stopped at the bare feet of a crouching boy, her tongue lolling.

The youngster cringed but didn't try to flee. Reed praised his dog, then met the gaze of the small, dark-haired teen. "Hello, Dominic. Where have you been?"

"I ain't…"

The purposeful scowl on Reed's face was enough to make the boy pause. "Yes, you are. Don't even try to lie to a police dog like my Jessie. She's never wrong." He held out the satiny jacket Kiera had given him earlier. "Lose this?"

"Maybe."

"Where's your girlfriend?"

"I got no girlfriend."

"Okay. Then where is Kiera Underhill? The three of us need to have a little chat."

Reed paused to radio news of Jessie's success and saw other officers begin to relax and return to their vehicles.

"Don't even think about running," he warned the fidgeting boy.

"Okay, okay. But it wasn't my fault."

"What wasn't? What happened here?"

"I-I heard somebody was down here asking about Snapper. I figured I'd get blamed for losing him so I split." He raised a hand as if taking an oath. "I didn't steal him. And I don't know where he is. The only reason I came back here is because I saw you and your dog going the other way."

Unconvinced, Reed pressed the question. "Suppose I believe you? How can you prove you're telling the truth?"

"Um, I don't know." The timbre of the boy's voice wavered from alto to soprano and back down again.

"Well, you'd better think of something, and quick," Reed said flatly. "If it was Snapper, there's no earthly reason for him to have wandered all the way down here by himself."

Dominic's dark eyes sparked. "Hey, I never said I found him here. Some guy gave him to me, back when I was still living in a foster home."

So, at least the kids had their story straight, not that he bought it. "Oh, yeah?" Reed said. "And where were you when this happened?"

He was fairly certain the boy was lying until he said, "Over by Vanderbilt Parkway. Queens."

Heart in his throat, Reed bent to stare into the teen's face, looking for clues that he'd made up his excuse. Deception might be this kid's modus operandi, but truth lay in his current expression.

"I can check your former foster placements, you know."

"Go ahead, man. Check. That's where I was when I got Snapper."

"So how did you wind up here?" Reed was hesitant to accept anything at face value. The department and his unit had chased down too many false reports and erroneous sightings for him to be easily satisfied.

"I ran away, all right? And I'll do it again if you try to send me back there. Those people hated Snapper. I promised I'd get a job to pay for his food but they wouldn't listen."

Softening his tone, Reed asked, "Did you have trouble getting him to eat?"

"How did you know?"

"Your friend Kiera mentioned it. There's a good reason. Snapper and all our dogs are taught to turn down food that isn't offered by their handlers or trainers. I'm surprised you got him to eat anything."

"Is that why he got so skinny? Man, that's twisted. He could've starved to death."

"I assume his survival instincts have kicked in by now. That's probably why he was okay finding his own dinner but balked when you kids tried to feed him. He still remembered his poison-proofing training."

"Hey! I didn't poison him. He was fine the last time I saw him. He just keeps running off, that's all."

Reed straightened, noting that Kiera and Abigail were lingering nearby. "So, where is he now?"

The skinny shoulders shrugged, then slumped. "Beats me. One day he's with me and the next he's gone. Nobody saw him go so I didn't know where to look besides around here." He sniffled. "Some stupid tourist probably took him."

"Tell me more about the guy you got him from in the first place? Can you remember what he looked like?" It was hard to keep from sounding too excited, given that there was a chance the boy had seen Jordan's killer.

"Sort of, I guess." Dominic's head bobbed up and down, his forehead knitting. "He was just a regular guy. Old, like you."

Reed snorted. "Got it. Do you think you could help a sketch artist draw his picture?"

"I might. What's in it for me?"

Fine, Reed thought, more than ready to barter. "Food. As much as you want for as long as these concessions stay open tonight. My treat."

"Seriously?"

"Seriously. I'm going to radio my headquarters with a report and ask an artist to meet us down here. That way you won't have to ride in a police car." *And I won't have to jump through so many technical, legal hoops*, he added to himself.

Abigail would probably volunteer to help, too,

Reed reasoned, making the boardwalk a perfect place to debrief the boy. If Dom kept playing it straight with the adults, Reed intended to feed him until he couldn't hold another bite.

Vanderbilt Parkway. Reed figured he'd never hear that name without remembering the shock they'd all felt when Jordy's body had been found. Images of that body were branded in Reed's brain as if made by a hot iron of sorrow.

God willing, the face of Jordy's possible killer held as firm a grip on the mind of the wiry teen. Dominic Walenski might be the only witness who could provide clues to the elusive murderer. No way was Reed letting him out of his sight until he had more answers.

Abigail spotted Dom when she caught sight of Reed. Jessie had done it! It took a monumental effort to stay where she was and make Kiera wait for Reed to finish talking to the boy.

A wave of Reed's arm and the helpful actions of other officers dispersed the crowd. Jessie was practically dancing, her tail up, her ears flapping and a knotted section of damp rope clamped between her teeth as her reward for a job well done. Reed, on the other hand, seemed almost morose. If the two teens hadn't been so close by, she would have immediately asked him why he wasn't as happy as everybody else, including his K-9.

Nevertheless, Abigail flashed a grin. Kiera might not have forgiven her for the chastisement over making a false police report, but she cared enough about Dominic to stick around. Good. One step at a time.

Despite the sour look Kiera got from the boy, Abigail continued to smile. "Good job, Jessie." She patted the broad, tan head, dodging the frayed end of the dog's reward toy before her gaze rose to meet Reed's and she added, "You, too, Officer Branson."

"Thanks." Although his expression remained sober, he did nod politely. "Dominic and I are going to go grab a late supper before the concessions close. You're invited."

"Thanks." Including Kiera seemed logical and smart, so Abigail looped an arm around each teen's shoulders and guided them toward the boardwalk. She didn't have to look back to know Reed and Jessie were following closely, because every second or third stride, the soggy rope brushed against her calf.

The kids were casting surreptitious glances at each other, clearly wishing a counselor was not walking between them. Well, tough. The thought of combining her efforts and Reed's gave Abigail hope of soothing tempers and learning more. All they had to do was foster a relaxed atmosphere and let these young people be themselves. Given their tenuous position as runaways and the way they viewed authority figures as the enemy, she and Reed had their work cut out for them.

She positioned herself on the outside of a small picnic table fronting a food stand and gestured to the teens. "Grab a seat, guys."

The look she got from Reed as he and his K-9 joined them was one of approval. Thanks to her, they were positioned to head off a dash to escape as well as clearly see each of the kids' faces. She gave him a smile. "I'll have one of their famous special hot dogs and a small soda."

He handed her the looped end of Jessie's leash, his gaze shifting from the dog to the teens as if reminding them it would be useless to try to run away. "What about the two of you? The same? I can always go back for seconds."

"Yeah, okay," Dominic said. Kiera nodded.

Abigail suspected that Jessie wouldn't do a thing about chasing anybody unless Reed gave her that specific command, but she pretended otherwise, grasping the leash tightly and acting as if she were the only reason the sweet bloodhound wasn't snarling and behaving like an attack dog. The ruse worked well enough that the teens seated across the table hardly moved a muscle.

Reed was back with their meal in minutes. He doled it out, reclaimed his K-9, then slid onto the bench closest to Dominic. "Okay. Eat. Then we'll talk."

Less hungry than she was curious, Abigail concentrated mostly on her companions. Reed remained tense. Kiera seemed relieved. The boy, though clearly starved and willing to eat, maintained a wary demeanor that she found strange. Of course, none of the kids was particularly fond of law enforcement because they were often apprehended and forced back into a system that, although designed to keep them safe and well, could easily fail. She knew that and clearly so did Reed, or he would have placed Dominic in official custody.

"I told you all I know," the boy muttered with his mouth half full.

"So, you said." Reed looked at Kiera. "What about you? Any chance you saw the guy who gave him Snapper?"

"Not me. I've been here all summer. Dom's kinda new."

"Is that why you lied to get us to come look for him?"

"Yeah, I guess."

Abigail saw the boy shoot Kiera a troubled glance. "*You* did this?" He muttered under his breath.

"Well, somebody had to," the girl replied. "We were worried about you."

"So you called the *cops*?" He was clearly annoyed. "Did you want 'em to arrest me for stealing the dog?"

"No, no!" Kiera insisted. Her meal was forgotten as she reached for his thin arm. "I didn't tell anybody about Snapper until they figured it out themselves." She began to smile as if enjoying a private joke. "I told 'em *you'd* been kidnapped."

Dom jumped back so forcefully he almost toppled off the bench. "You *what*?"

"It's okay. They know it was a fib. I just wanted to make them take me seriously and come look for you."

Expecting an explosion of angry words, Abigail was astounded to see the wiry teen overcome with what looked like fear. His hands gripped the edge of the table. His complexion blanched. His dark eyes widened and glistened as if he might be about to cry. His jaw dropped but no sound came out.

The instant she turned and looked at Reed's face, she knew that something crucial was happening. She just didn't know what it was. Or how to help.

* * *

Reed waited as he watched the boy's emotional upheaval. It was clear Dominic was hiding something, and although it probably didn't have anything to do with Jordy's murder, it was evidently frightening. Kiera had inadvertently scared the socks off her younger friend and it was Reed's duty to get past his facade of street courage and pull the details out of him.

And protect him, Reed added to himself. That kid was scared speechless. Biding his time, he took a bite of the hot dog he'd bought for himself, noting that he was the only one still eating. The girl looked confused, Abigail was obviously puzzled, and Dominic acted as if he was about to be sentenced to death row. Anything that serious called for finesse.

"You do know you're safe sitting here with me, right?" Reed said casually.

Dom was staring into the distance, his eyes shining, reflecting the overhead lights. When he shook his head, the spots of color glimmered.

"That's why I'm sticking with Officer Branson," Abigail explained.

When Kiera gave a derisive snort, Dominic's head snapped around. His expression was so poignant the girl shrugged and asked, "What?"

"Nothing." He was staring at his food but had stopped eating.

"Hmm." Reed took another bite, then washed it down with his own soda before concentrating on Kiera. "That was pretty smart of you to mention kidnapping. What gave you the idea?"

"Like I said, I wanted you cops to pay attention."

"Well, it worked." He paused. "So, why is your friend so mad at you? You must have some idea."

"Naw." She folded her arms in an expression of defense. "I don't have a clue. Maybe he's just a big baby."

"I am not!" marked the boy's return to the conversation.

Kiera shrugged. "Whatever."

Silence followed. Reed watched and waited. Both young people were fidgeting, making him wonder if their angst was for the same reason or if each had a separate secret. Dominic seemed unduly upset about Kiera's subterfuge while the girl was acting clueless. Either she was a great actress or she truly didn't know why her friend was so angry.

Suddenly, Kiera gaped. She stared at the boy as if willing him to explain. But what? What had passed between the two runaways that he had missed? A quick glance at Abigail's frown told him she was as confused as he was.

Dominic gave a barely perceptible nod. That

led to Kiera's exclamation of, "No!" followed by a grab at his hand. The boy's brown eyes filled with tears. His nod continued, gaining strength until his mop of dark hair flopped forward, masking the upper half of his face.

Whisperings between the two young people were lost in the noise of the crowds near the concession tables. Reed though he'd managed to pick out a few key words but there was no way to grasp the full meaning of the exchange without more detail. He did know that Kiera was now apparently as frightened as Dom, which might help once there was an actual crime to investigate.

"You can't stay here anymore," Kiera said flatly before switching to address the adults, particularly Reed. "You have to put him in protective custody."

He couldn't help smiling. "I think you watch too much television. Protective custody is only for innocent victims who can prove they are really in danger."

Kiera was on her feet in a flash. She grabbed Dominic's arm, jerked him off the bench and started to drag him away.

The boy didn't protest verbally but he did make a grab for his soda cup.

"Leave it," Kiera shouted. "We're out of here!"

FOURTEEN

Abigail was so startled she almost tumbled backward off the bench. When she regained her balance and looked over at Reed, he and Jessie were already on the move.

They zigzagged between tables, cleared the edge of the red-and-yellow canvas awning and disappeared among the milling vacationers and locals. There was no way she'd be able to catch any of them at this point, so she cleared off the table, dumped their trash and paced, waiting for one or more of her former companions to return.

An overview of people nearby proved unproductive. Not only was there no sign of Kiera's close friends, Abigail didn't spot any of the kids who were regulars at AFS, either. A few young adult males did look slightly familiar, however. That was a bit of a surprise. Most of the kids who aged out of the state foster care program, as well as her privately funded one, could hardly wait to leave the area once they turned eighteen.

It never ceased to amaze her that many of them who could have signed on to stay in the system longer failed to do so. Not only would it have helped them find a good job, they would have had support.

"I should know about poor choices," she murmured to herself. In her day, she'd almost let her pride cause her to miss a chance to get a higher education. Thankfully, the part-time job she'd been directed toward in her mid-teens had led to meeting mentors who had helped her turn her life around. Now she was dedicated to doing the same for others, like Kiera and Dominic.

Speaking of which... Reed's height helped her spot him before she could see who was by his side. Sadly, Kiera wasn't with Dominic any more. Oh, well, of the two, the boy was undoubtedly more in need of aid than the more street savvy girl was.

The crowd didn't exactly part for the police officer the way the Red Sea had for Moses in biblical times, but Reed's strength of presence seemed to cause quite a few human obstacles to give ground.

Dominic came into full view. Abigail studied his face, his body language. At first, he seemed resigned, then tense, then quickly scared to death. As far as she could tell, nothing about their surroundings had changed, yet the boy was obviously affected negatively.

She stepped close to Reed as soon as he'd cleared the throng. "Something is very wrong."

"Yeah. I lost your girl."

"No, no. That's not what I mean." Abigail cupped a hand around her mouth and stood on tiptoe to explain as privately as possible. "It's not Kiera I'm worried about right now, it's this one. You couldn't see the funny look that just came over him but I could. He's terrified. We need to get him away from here."

"You're serious?"

"Yes. I'll take responsibility. We need to go someplace quiet and safe. ASAP."

"All right. If you say so."

She fell into step on the opposite side of the boy, consciously guarding him. Until this second, she'd been so worried about Dominic and Kiera, she'd forgotten the bit of lost memory she'd uncovered.

"By the way," Abigail said, "waiting for you I had a surprising flash of insight into the men who grabbed me. One was masked to begin with. He had a round face and big, rough hands. The other one wasn't quite as large, the way I first thought. He had a face like a weasel and I think he was younger. I know he was skinnier."

To her delight, Reed looked pleased. "Wonderful. Let's go back to my car and wait for the sketch artist. You can make use of him after our friend here is done."

"I—I'm not sure I remember their faces that well," she hedged. "It's one thing to get an over-all impression of them and altogether different to be able to pick out individual characteristics."

"At least you can give it a try. Right?"

She cast a sidelong glance at Dominic, ruing her thoughtless comments and hoping he wasn't going to adopt the same defeatist attitude regarding the man who had given him Snapper. It was too late to take back her candid remarks, but she might be able to counteract their deleterious effect.

"Of course I'll try. And once I've started to see the faces develop, I'll be able to make adjustments to get them just right."

"That's the spirit," Reed said. Although his voice sounded pleasant and enthusiastic, Abigail could tell his speech was as much for the boy's sake as hers had been. They both knew they were walking a tightrope here, balancing between what the law allowed and what her office could do. The main goal was, as always, the ultimate well-being of the street kids. She knew from experience that many of them were repeat runaways and would take off again the minute they felt threatened or abused or simply didn't like listening to parental-type authority figures.

She intended to treat Dominic equitably, yet she wasn't above giving him more leeway than usual if doing so led to the arrest of criminals and the solving of crimes.

One thing was certain. The German shepherd the youngster had been given was crucially important to Reed. If she was putting the pieces of this story together correctly, the person Dominic had met when he'd accepted Snapper could be connected to the untimely demise of Reed's boss, Snapper's former handler.

That wasn't simple dog-napping.

That was murder.

As soon as he had convinced Dominic that he wasn't under arrest and had talked him into climbing into the SUV, it was easy to load Abigail and his K-9. Reed radioed headquarters and explained his change of plans. He didn't want to panic the kid more than he already was, so he refrained from giving specific reasons for the relocation of the rendezvous with the police artist. Now that he'd had time to observe the Walenski boy more carefully, he agreed with Abigail. Something besides being with a cop had the kid spooked. Judging by the way he kept peering out of the windows and scanning the passing crowd, he was plenty scared of whoever he thought was out there.

It occurred to Reed to put Jessie in the back seat with Dom, and he would have if not for the artist's imminent arrival. With the AC running and everybody safe, he waited outside his vehicle, ready to flag down whichever artist showed up.

As he saw an approaching patrol unit slowing, he raised his hand to wave. The car pulled up beside his, hazard lights blinking. Reed reached to hold the passenger door as it opened and was pleasantly surprised to see the unit's ace tech guru, curly-haired, blonde Danielle Abbott, step out.

"Danielle! I assumed Joey Calderone would be assigned. Are you acting as my sketch artist tonight?" Danielle was not only a tech genius, she was also incredibly talented at digital art, particularly faces, and sometimes acted as a backup for Calderone.

She pushed her large, round-framed glasses up the bridge of her nose with one finger. "Sure am." Handing him her laptop and a red tote filled to bursting with who knew what, she flashed a wide grin. "Calderone was out of town so I volunteered. I've been dying to try my new face-building program in the field."

"This may work out for the best. My reporting party is a scared kid." Reed grinned. "If anybody can put him at ease and coax out the information we need, it's you."

She gathered a handful of curls at her nape before pulling an alligator clip out of the pocket of her flowery sundress. "Hang on a sec while I pin up my hair. I thought it'd be cooler at the beach but it's still too hot for me."

"September has its moments," Reed replied. He eyed his parked car. "I'll introduce you and leave you with the boy. His name is Dominic Walenski. He's been in foster care and has a record of running away, so don't let him trick you. The most important thing is finding out what the perp looked like who gave him Snapper."

Her wide eyes looked enormous behind the large lenses. "Snapper? You found him?"

"Not yet, but I'm hoping we'll soon have an idea what Jordy's killer looks like."

Danielle pressed a hand to her clavicle and gasped. "Whoa! Okay, sure. Let me at him."

"Easy," Reed warned. "We think something else is bothering Dominic right now and I don't want you to spook him, okay?"

"Yeah, yeah. I'll be cool." She seemed to be struggling to control her excitement. "Are you sure the person who had Snapper was the murderer?"

"No." Reed shook his head. "But it's the strongest lead we've had since the guy who planted Chief Jameson's fake suicide note was killed. We have to start somewhere."

"Gotcha. Who's in there besides your witness?" She was peering through the windows of Reed's SUV.

"That's Abigail Jones." He decided to withhold details that were not pertinent to the case. "She works in Brighton Beach and along this part of the shore with kids like Dom. I thought her presence might settle him down if she kept us company."

One of the tech wizard's perfectly limned eyebrows arched and she gave Reed a mischievous glance. "Whatever you say, Branson. Just remember what's happened to some of the other K-9 cops recently. Zack Jameson, Luke Hathaway and Finn Gallagher, for instance. Love is in the air, my friend."

He huffed. "The only thing in this air is the smell of popcorn, hot dogs and suntan lotion, so don't go imagining things, Abbott."

"Hey, can I help it if I'm a hopeless romantic?" She sobered again. "You interrupted my date tonight, you know."

"Sorry. You look nice in that dress," Reed told her, meaning it.

He saw the woman's sharp mind zero in on reality and heard her sigh. "It's okay. I know what's most important, same as you. We'll get justice for Jordan—and for poor Katie." A deeper sigh. "I can't imagine losing a husband, especially while being pregnant. She has to be going crazy with worry."

"You know the Jamesons are looking after her," he countered. "It's really a good thing they shared that multifamily Rego Park house to begin with."

"Still sad." The loose curls framing Danielle's face followed the shaking of her head. "It's hard to imagine how the whole family feels. Those brothers were close."

"Well, at least they didn't lose Carter, too," Reed said, recalling the officer's recent leg wound. "He's on the mend."

"From your lips to God's ears," she said, brightening and stepping past him. "Let's go meet this whiz kid so I can get started."

To Abigail's surprise and chagrin, she felt a twinge of jealousy when a pretty blonde got out of the other police car and stood speaking with Reed so intently.

What is wrong with me? He can talk to any-body he pleases. It's no business of mine. And yet, in some unfathomable way, her life had become intrinsically connected to Reed's. She could already sense his emotions, predict his responses. That wasn't natural. Not at all. At least not in respect to the handsome police officer. Most kids she could read like a book, even when they were mixed up with drugs or petty crimes or lying to her face. In Reed's case, however, the connection went deeper. Empathy explained some of it, of course. She accepted that. She shared his disappointment when plans didn't come together perfectly, such as when their vehicle had been wrecked.

Mulling over her situation as he and the other woman approached the SUV, Abigail felt a tug on her heart that was so poignant it almost made her gasp. Only the presence of the impressionable boy kept her from fully acknowledging her feelings. She cared about this man so deeply, so totally, she could hardly breathe.

The conclusion that shot into her mind as if fired from a gun was undeniable. *Impossible.* Yet true. Like it or not, she had fallen in love with K-9 officer Reed Branson almost overnight. That was crazy. He hadn't even kissed her. How could she possibly have fallen for him?

Making the best use of the moments before he reached her door, Abigail covered her face with both hands and prayed silently, asking God for insight into her own mind, her obvious confusion.

The door lock clicked. Reed was standing

there. Abigail met his quizzical expression. "You okay?" he asked casually.

"Fine, fine. Just tired." She swung her feet out and stood.

"This is our tech wizard, Danielle Abbott," Reed said. "Danielle, meet Abigail Jones."

"A real pleasure." The amply endowed blonde extended a bejeweled hand.

Abigail accepted the gesture and shook hands. "Thank you for coming on such short notice." A slight eye movement indicated the boy in the back seat. "Dominic is ready to help us. As soon as you're through and satisfied with the face he chooses, I've promised him ice cream. Two scoops." She looked to Reed. "I hope you don't mind."

He smiled. "Not at all. You can sit with Danielle and do your faces while Dom and I go get his treat."

"Her, too?" the tech expert asked.

Abigail answered for Reed. "Yes. Me, too. I've been having some trouble recalling an incident in my past and had a flash of insight tonight. I suppose I'd better try to make something concrete out of it before it slips away again."

All business, Danielle gave Abigail the once-over. "So, you're the one."

"I beg your pardon?"

Danielle's smile returned. "We've heard plenty

about a pretty assault victim our confirmed bachelor here has been keeping company with. Now I'm even more pleased to meet you."

It was all Abigail could do to keep from scowling at both of them. So she was the subject of gossip around their police station. "Terrific. It's good to hear that I've given you all something to talk about. Now, if you don't mind, Dominic needs to get started."

"Oops, sorry." Danielle shot a brief glance at Reed. "I didn't mean to make trouble, buddy."

"Not a problem," he said flatly. "I'm a big boy. I can take a little ribbing. Just be sure you explain that this is work, not play, when you go back to headquarters."

"Work. Got it." The wink the blonde gave Reed was so blatant it made Abigail's blood boil. Talk about getting an immediate answer to a prayer for clearer thinking. Reed not only still classified her as a job and nothing more, he was openly flirting with a woman he obviously admired.

Sending thanks heavenward for such clear enlightenment was called for, Abigail knew. But right then and there, watching the way Reed and Danielle looked at each other, she was incapable of genuine gratitude.

"Ask and you shall receive," Abigail quoted to herself, wondering why she felt even worse

after getting a definite response to her prayer-
ful appeal.

As she watched Danielle join Dom in the back
seat, Abigail found a trace of humor in the irony
of her situation and whispered one more short
prayer.

"Um, Father, do you suppose I could have do-
overs and take back that last prayer?"

FIFTEEN

"I think we should take him home with us," Reed told Abigail. "I've talked to my chief and he's left it up to me for the present."

"Take Dominic home? Why?"

"Because it makes sense. There's no way to keep him safe when he's wandering all over the beach." He tried to subdue a smile and ended up with a quirky grin. "Look at it as informal protective custody."

"Kiera got to you, didn't she?"

"Maybe a little."

"If you keep taking lost souls home with you, you'll run out of house space."

Noting the rosy glow of her cheeks beneath the cute freckles, he reassured her. "They're not all lost. You're not. You just need a little TLC until you regain your memory." Reed's smile widened. "And it's working. You've already had two incidents that show recovery."

"Identifying that pizza man's voice was a mistake."

"I wasn't counting him. Give yourself credit, Abigail. You're a smart, intelligent, capable woman. You'll pull it together. I know you will."

"Yeah, right," she mumbled. Then louder, "I wish I'd known somebody like you when I was Dom's age."

Assuming a relaxed pose, Reed tried to draw her out. "Oh? Was it really that bad?"

For an instant he was afraid he'd angered her, because she seemed to be struggling emotionally. When she shook her head and said, "No, it was worse," his heart clenched. How could anybody hurt a kid, particularly a sweet one like Abigail had surely been?

Although she folded her arms across her chest and lifted her chin with evident pride, he could tell she was feeling vulnerable, so he stopped asking questions in the hopes she'd voluntarily reveal more about herself. He didn't realize he'd been holding his breath until she began to speak.

"I don't remember my father," she said. "That wouldn't have been so bad if Mom hadn't brought home so many new daddies for me to learn to love. When I was little it was easy to get used to them but as I got older and began to look…" She blushed. "You know. Pretty soon I was staying out late or not going home at all just to keep from having to dodge unwelcome advances from strange men."

"Your mother permitted this?"

"My mother was rarely sober. I doubt she noticed much. When I finally hit the streets for keeps at sixteen, I'm not even sure she reported me missing."

Reed gently touched her shoulder. "I'm so sorry."

"Hey, I lived through it. And it led to the start of my career in public service. If I could get squared away and turn out okay, it's proof some of these other runaways can do the same. That's what I tell them if I think they need that kind of encouragement."

"Good for you."

"Good for the people and organizations that were there for me, you mean. I didn't do it alone." She began to smile slightly, a dreamy look in her eyes that made them glisten in the neon flashes from nearby businesses and concessions. "I was really struggling, despite everything, until a mentor dragged me to a church youth meeting. It wasn't at all like I'd thought church would be. The music was upbeat, the snacks were great and nobody looked down on me."

"I know what you mean. I used to belong to a group like that. Mine even passed out free Bibles."

"Then you do understand. I'd never heard Jesus presented the way those kids did it. They talked about Him as if they actually knew Him personally, and I wanted the same relationship. It was after I committed my life to Him that things began to make sense." She huffed. "I don't mean all my troubles vanished. Getting it together took time and a lot of work. But I think I've managed to forgive my mother. She was a victim, too."

"I agree." Reed set aside the last vestiges of concern about his professional image and reached out to her. It was as natural an act as breathing, although once Abigail was in his arms, he did have a little trouble catching his breath.

At first she seemed reluctant, but in seconds she had relaxed into a shared embrace. Others on the sidewalk passed them by as if they were invisible. Coney Island was that kind of place, a place where romantic couples met and mingled with crowds of like-minded revelers, all intent on making the most of the last warm days of autumn.

Tucking Abigail against him, he rested his chin on the top of her head, feeling the tickle of her hair, the whisper of her warm breath. He knew he should have been shocked when his mind had so easily provided the word "romantic" in connection to what was happening between them. Somehow, he wasn't even remotely surprised.

He drew a shaky, deep breath and released it slowly, admitting how much he cared for her and wondering what in the world he was going to do about it. This situation was akin to a hapless swimmer being caught in a riptide and pulled out over his depth. Way over.

That wouldn't have been so bad if he hadn't viewed himself as the lifeguard on duty.

Standing there, encircled by Reed's arms, Abigail closed her eyes and let herself absorb his strength, his support. Clearly her story had touched him, and of that she was glad. What remained puzzling was why, once he had offered solace, he continued to hold her. Not that she was complaining. No, sir. Given a choice she'd be glad to stand right there with her arms around him for as long as possible.

There was a very slight loosening of Reed's arms, a subtle easing away. Feeling that change, Abigail had no choice but to let go and step back. She forced a smile and gazed up, hoping she didn't look as if she were mooning over him.

"Thanks," she said. "I don't talk about my past often. Every time I do, it takes a lot out of me."

"I understand. Better now?"

The rumble of his voice seemed to convey more than concern. If she hadn't heard the sketch artist mention his confirmed bachelorhood, she might have imagined that they shared the same tender emotions she'd recently been battling against.

"Yes, thanks." Abigail let her gaze drift over the passing pedestrians without conscious thought. How long had she been denying her burgeoning affection for this special man? It was impossible to tell, probably because her psyche had been so frail to begin with. And now that she was healing? She huffed. Now that her normal sensibilities were returning, she supposed she should concentrate on self-determination and the pride of being her own person. It had taken years to mature to that point. She didn't want to abandon the courageous self she'd discovered and nurtured. It was what kept her together and gave her the strength to help others.

That was the trouble with falling in love, she mused. A person had to relinquish too much. Look at what had happened to her poor mother when she'd tried to rely on a man to complete her and had failed over and over.

Well, that pattern wasn't going to repeat itself in Abigail Jones. No way. As soon as she'd recovered enough to more fully describe the men who had attacked her, she and Reed would probably never see each other again.

Given the unwelcome reaction of her heart to that fact, she figured the sooner they parted the better. Yes, she was going to miss seeing him, being near him. But that didn't mean there was anything personal going on. He'd put it best when he'd instructed Danielle. They all needed to remember that he was merely doing his job.

Standing straight, shoulders back, Abigail left him and started toward the parked SUV. As soon as Dominic was finished she was going to take his place and describe the faces from her hazy memory. This was not the time to give up or give in. She was going to succeed or else.

Failure was not an option.

Reed hung back and let her go, knowing that nobody in his right mind would threaten her while she was standing next to a police car.

He'd been a fool to touch Abigail again, let alone embrace her, yet he'd been unable to stop himself. Every fiber of his being had cried out, insisting he offer comfort, and he had yielded. He must never step out of line like that again. It didn't matter how he felt personally, it was wrong of him to take advantage of her vulnerabilities. Later, when she was fully recovered and back to living a normal life, maybe he'd change his mind and ask her for a date, but right here, right now, he needed to keep his distance.

"As if that's going to be easy," Reed muttered. "I am in so deep already I can't believe it."

He saw her looking back. Watching him. Good thing she wasn't a lip reader.

Seeking something to do besides stand there and waste time, he decided to let Jessie out for a little exercise. To his chagrin, Abigail stepped back and seemed to tense up more when he approached.

He flashed his best fake grin. "Just checking on my four-footed partner. We won't go far. I'm keeping an eye on you."

She returned an equally forced smile. "Okay. I'm sure it will be my turn with the sketch artist soon."

"There's nothing to worry about," Reed told her, opening the rear hatch and liberating his leashed K-9. "Danielle will walk you through it. You'll do fine."

"Right." Sobering, Abigail made a face. "It seems like the harder I try to bring those faces back, the less I actually remember about them."

"Then think about something else until it's time to work for real. It'll come to you more easily if you don't force it."

Before Abigail had time to reply, there was a tapping on the window behind her. Reed hit the release on his key fob to unlock the door, and Dominic bounded out. "Ice cream!"

"Gotcha." Reed held up his keys for Abigail. "Climb in. The door will lock by itself. If you need to get out before I get back, use my keys." He tossed part of the ring to her. "Don't lose that or we'll have to walk home."

He waited until she was safely locked in the SUV before he turned to his young companion and pointed toward the boardwalk. "Let's go. We don't want the ice cream stand to close before we get there."

"Yay! Two scoops. Chocolate."

"Coming right up."

Reed followed the boy's zigzag path between groups of people, staying close and keeping Jessie on a short lead. Later, he'd ask how the session with Danielle had gone. While Dominic was acting carefree and happy, he was going to let him enjoy himself as much as possible.

Reed chuckled. Too bad ice cream wasn't enough to lift Abigail's spirits or he'd buy out the whole stand for her.

Danielle was easier to work with than Abigail had expected. She started with basic head shapes and added facial details with simple keystrokes until there was no more adjusting to do.

Danielle held up her laptop. "Well? What do you think?"

"The skinny one is pretty close. I'm sorry I couldn't be more helpful with the bigger man. He had a mask on when I first saw him, and I was pretty traumatized later."

"Not to worry. These guys run in packs like wolves. Locate one and chances are his buddies won't be hard to find." She reached out and patted Abigail's arm. "You doing okay?"

A shrug. "I guess so. Just disappointed."

"Don't be. You did great. I'll send this image to headquarters and make sure all the patrol units get emailed copies. It's a big city but we have eyes everywhere. We'll turn him up."

"I hope so. I've been too nervous to leave my apartment. If Reed—Officer Branson—hadn't encouraged me, I'd still be stuck there, staring at the walls and jumping every time somebody knocked on my door."

"He's a good cop. A good man. Our unit has had enough grief to last us all a lifetime and we'd hate to see another member hurt, if you get my meaning."

Abigail blinked rapidly. Had this stranger somehow glimpsed the truth and become concerned she'd break Reed's heart?

"I'd never lead any man on if I wasn't going to follow through," Abigail promised. "There really isn't anything between Reed and me. Honest. He's just helping out."

"Okay. If you say so." She smiled, and her eyes twinkled behind the large lenses of her designer frames. "Let me give you one of my cards. That way, if you do recall more and Reed isn't around, you can reach me directly."

If Reed isn't around? Was it possible? Of course it was. There wasn't even a slim possibility that he was going to keep shepherding her up and down the boardwalk, let alone allow her to live with him and his sister for much longer. It would behoove her to keep that in mind above all else.

She glanced at the loathsome face staring back at her from the laptop screen. "Will you email a copy of that to me, too, please? I want to be able to show it to my boss in case he comes around my office. We both need to be prepared."

"Will do. You ready for your ice cream treat?"

That brought a real smile. "You think I need bribing?"

"Nope," Danielle replied, hitting the button on the key to unlock the doors. "But I do. I was supposed to be eating lobster and steak with a good-looking hunk about now. The least Branson can do is buy me a cone."

Stepping out first, Abigail felt as if a heavy load had lifted, physically and emotionally. Directing the formation of that little weasel's nasty face had helped release part of the burden she'd been carrying. Being out from under that weight was a big relief.

Providing I'm right, she told herself, sensing the mantle of peace slipping slightly. Had she seen that face somewhere else and imagined it belonging to her attacker? She'd been so positive while in the car, yet doubt was creeping in as the seconds passed.

She hesitated, frowning. "What if I'm wrong? What if the person I described is innocent? I don't want to blame someone who doesn't deserve it."

"Let us sort that out," Danielle said. "It's your job to do as well as possible and our job to take it from there."

"Right. Thanks." With a sideways nod she indicated which direction they should go. "I know where the guys probably went. Come on. Let's surprise them."

As Abigail's gaze passed over the crowd, her subconscious gave her a start. *Whoa! Was that...? No way.* She had to be hallucinating after the recent sketch session. There was no other explanation why someone would look so familiar. Unless...

She turned and grabbed her companion's arm. "Look. Over my shoulder. Do you see him?"

"Who?"

"The guy in my sketch. He's standing by the ticket booth." The look on Danielle's face wasn't comforting. "You see him, don't you?"

Golden curls bobbed and earrings swung as the other woman said, "Sorry."

Abigail whirled. There was nobody around who even remotely resembled the person she'd described. So why was her pulse running wild and her mouth as dry as beach sand in July?

Chin up, she stood tall and reclaimed the shred of peace remaining, figuratively wrapping herself in hopes of anonymity. Maybe she had made a mistake. It was certainly possible. But that didn't mean she wasn't going to become complacent.

He was out there somewhere.

She could feel the menace.

And someday soon she was going to spot him for real.

SIXTEEN

The drive back to Queens seemed to fly by for Reed, undoubtedly because his brain was occupied by more than safe driving.

A glance in the mirror told him that the boy and dog had fallen asleep sharing the rear seat. Dom had one arm over Jessie's shoulders, his head pillowed on the K-9's soft fur.

Just to be certain, Reed cleared his throat before speaking. Nobody except Abigail paid the slightest attention. If he told her what he suspected, would it make matters worse or better? There was no way to tell. As he saw it, knowing to be cautious was the lesser of two evils.

"I was studying that face you and Danielle came up with," he began. "Something about him looked familiar."

Reed saw her eyes widen, her lips part as if she might gasp.

Instead, she said, "I thought so, too. Do you

think I subconsciously described somebody else we saw on the boardwalk?"

"Not necessarily. That was where you were when you were attacked. Maybe the original thugs were hanging around and decided to come closer to check you out. See what you remembered."

"That's not a very comforting idea."

"No, but it can be a useful warning."

"Surely they won't try anything again. Not while I'm with you and Jessie."

"You're right." He wanted to reassure her without making her worry. "But life has to go on, Abigail. I won't always be close by. That's why it's so important for you to keep remembering more about your ordeal."

"I know, I know. You don't have to beat me over the head with it. Don't you think I'm doing the best I can?" She looked contrite before adding, "Sorry. It's not your fault."

He paused to regroup. "I was trying to explain that this isn't my regular area of coverage. The K-9s in my unit move all over the city, go to wherever we're needed most. I could be called away at any time. I want you to promise you'll stay aware of your surroundings and be very cautious."

She humphed. "Hey, I was doing fine hiding out in my apartment until you made me leave."

"Circumstances made you leave, not me," Reed countered. "You know that as well as I do. And while we're on the subject, what do you make of Kiera's panic earlier? When she got scared, grabbed the boy and took off, she was white as a sheet."

Abigail eyed the sleeping duo in the rear seat. "He knows what's going on. He must. Do you think we can persuade him to tell us'?"

"I'm not sure. Getting him to describe the guy who may have killed my chief was a big step."

Abigail gave a cynical chuckle. "Hey, convincing him to step foot inside this vehicle in the first place was giant. I thought we were going to lose him right then."

"It's thanks to you and Danielle that we didn't," Reed reminded her. "If I had been the only adult around he might not have agreed to anything."

"You've read his file?"

Reed nodded solemnly. "Yeah. He's all alone in the world. Little wonder he won't settle down in foster care. He has nothing left to go home to so he probably doesn't see the advantage of good behavior."

"Exactly." She leaned a little closer, making Reed's pulse jump. "Can I see the picture he came up with?"

"Sure." Hitting a key on the system in the

center console, he displayed the criminal's face on a screen.

"He looks enormous. Beefy. But I suppose any adult male would look gigantic to a boy Dom's size."

"Probably. Still, it's a start. The image has already gone out to all units and been posted at every precinct."

"I hope and pray you catch him."

Hearing pathos in her voice, Reed replied, "I wish we could jail them all and throw away the keys. Sometimes I wonder if we're even gaining ground. It's ridiculous to imagine getting every scrap of dirt swept up, so to speak, but I can dream."

To his surprise, she smiled. "You'd better not wipe out all the crime in New York. If you do, you'll be out of a job."

"I don't think there's much chance of that," Reed said. "So, how are you feeling after your session with Danielle? I didn't want to ask while she was around."

"The session wasn't nearly as satisfying as the ice cream afterward," Abigail said. "I just wish Kiera had been with us."

"She'll turn up soon," Reed promised. "As long as she's more worried about other kids than she is about herself, she'll come back." Once more he checked the rear seat. Thankfully, nothing had changed since the last time he'd looked.

"That speaks well of her," Abigail ventured. "If she were more self-centered, I'd see less chance of helping her learn to live a normal life."

"The way you do?"

That made her laugh again. "Um, yeah, well, let's reserve judgment on that subject until I remember the rest of the details of my attack, shall we? Right now, nothing feels normal to me."

Reed almost snorted in self-disgust. Instead, he said, "Yeah, well, there's a lot of that attitude going around."

Home, to Abigail, was still her empty apartment, and she desperately wanted to return to it for the solace found there. However, since Dominic was now a part of their little displaced group, she felt obligated to remain with Lani and Reed, at least for the time being.

What surprised her was Reed showing up at breakfast the next morning in his uniform.

"I've been called in to work," he told his sister, Abigail and Dominic. "They need Jessie, so we'll be gone today."

Lying under the table, the bloodhound thumped her tail on the floor while the black Lab pup chewed a squeaky toy.

Lani reached over and gave Reed a playful

punch in the shoulder. "You're obviously irre-placeable. I'll be glad when I get a dog of my own to partner."

Grateful for a benign topic of conversation, Abigail asked, "How long have you been a police officer?"

"Not quite long enough to be assigned a dog," the slightly younger woman answered. "But it won't be long now. I can hardly wait."

"Too bad Midnight isn't qualified." Hearing her name called, the pup began to paw at Abigail's knee, then switched to pulling on her shoe-laces until he had them untied.

"Yes, you," Abigail said, grinning. "Stop that. Bad."

"Clip her leash on her collar so you have control," Reed said. "Then you can give corrections properly. Timing is everything. She won't know what she's done wrong unless you correct immediately."

"Okay. Sorry. There's a lot to learn, isn't there?"

"You'll catch on," Lani assured her. "Just be consistent and if you're not sure, ask. I'll be glad to coach you while Reed's gone today."

"Will do. At least Midnight will keep me occupied until I go back to work full-time." Thoughts of resuming her job gave her the shivers. She'd have to accept Reed's offer of a ride.

Being shut up in a train car with strangers pushing in on her from every side was the stuff of nightmares.

Reed rose and carried his plate and coffee mug to the sink. "Gotta go. See you all later."

Abigail knew she was going to miss him something awful despite not being totally alone, but there was no way she'd let on. Whether Reed sensed her angst or not was a mystery. Part of her hoped he did while another part wanted to keep those inappropriate sentiments private.

Catching his eye as he donned his gear, she smiled, hoping he'd reciprocate. Instead, she got a look that bordered on an unspoken warning right before he said, "Stay here and stay inside unless Lani is with you and keep an eye on Dom."

That was so clearly an order, she bristled. Nevertheless, she said, "Okay, okay. I get it."

Did he really think her troubles would follow her all the way to his house? That seemed highly unlikely. Although there had been a prowler at her apartment, the police had never proved who he was or why he'd broken in. It could just as easily have been an isolated incident. After all, the prowler hadn't tried to harm her when he'd had the chance. He could have been a total stranger. As Reed had said, they were a long way from ending crime in the city.

And she'd been of little help, particularly if her facial reconstruction had been of someone other than her original attacker. She visualized the thin, menacing face. Those squinty eyes. The bad teeth and lips that seemed ready to snarl like a rabid dog. His was a hard face to forget.

While she helped Lani clear the table, Abigail tried to pull her mind away from negatives and enjoy watching Dominic wrestle on the living room floor with Midnight. A half-grown boy and a rambunctious puppy were meant for each other. It was hard to imagine either of them becoming mature, productive members of society, yet that was her aim. It had to be. If her hard road in life had shown her anything, it was that redemption was not only possible, it was a worthwhile goal.

Left alone, without proper intervention, anybody could become a criminal, even the most tenderhearted people. Kiera was a prime example. At this stage of life she could go either way. She still cared about others. But she also looked out for number one. When a crisis came, would she choose the right fork in the road or barrel down the wrong one into the oblivion of drugs or other unspeakable acts?

Picturing the girl and recalling her attitude toward authority, Abigail felt her own stomach clench. She looked around the Branson kitchen and living room. Framed family pictures on the walls and a homey feeling weren't enough to take the place of Reed's actual presence.

His leaving had left a void despite it being temporary. For no logical reason she was scared. Again. Abigail shivered, glancing at Lani and hoping to draw comfort.

Instead, the other woman was drying her hands and peering out the window over the sink.

Abigail was hardly able to ask, "What is it? What do you see?"

"Not sure." Lani laid aside the damp towel and opened a nearby drawer. Her hand closed around the grip of a handgun. She pulled a clip from a higher cupboard and loaded, chambering a round while aiming at the ceiling and continuing to monitor the small fenced yard.

No one had to tell Abigail to step back and keep her head down. She was getting all too used to strategic avoidance.

Hunched over, she hurried toward the boy and puppy, wondering how in the world she was going to protect them when the only weapon *she* possessed was her wits.

If Lani hadn't been home with Abigail and Dominic, Reed didn't know how he'd have coped. Yes, the chances of trouble at his house were slim. He knew that. He also knew that Abigail's nemesis had struck unexpectedly before. Right now, however, he had other concerns.

A bank in Brooklyn had been robbed and witnesses reported one of the thieves had escaped on foot. Jessie followed his trail as far as an alley, then lost the scent.

"Looks like he caught a ride," Reed reported via radio. "We'll be ten-ninety-nine, available in a couple of minutes."

He allowed his dog to carry her reward toy as they backtracked. That was the trouble with this job. Not every task ended in definitive success. It was his duty to not only direct his K-9 partner but to also keep up her spirits. She had to be made to feel some accomplishment or she might become depressed over her failure.

"Kind of like I feel about Abigail's stalker," he muttered in disgust. Jessie looked up at him, her eyes questioning, her tail still. "Yes, you're a good girl," Reed assured her. "A good, good dog."

That obviously pleased her because the spring in her step returned and she paced happily at his side, wagging vigorously enough to cause bystanders to step back and give them extra room.

Normally, Reed was as eager as his K-9 partner to respond to an incident. This was who he was, what he did. His identity. And yet today, all he wanted was to be released and make his way back to Queens. To his home. To Abigail.

Like it or not, he kept having disturbing thoughts about her safety. Lani was home and would watch over her and the boy, he knew, so he should have been satisfied. Well, he wasn't. Not even close. The same instinct that often kept him alive in dark alleys and dangerous neighborhoods was currently prickling the short hair on the nape of his neck and sending shivers along his spine.

Pausing just short of the patrol cars grouped in front of the bank, he pulled out his cell phone. A quick call to his sister would put his mind at ease.

Although he wanted to phone Abigail instead, he figured Lani would be more inclined to deliver the kind of clear status report he craved.

The phone rang. And rang. And rang.

Reed stared at his phone, wondering if he'd pressed the wrong button. He hadn't. Maybe his sister was outside with Abigail and Midnight and didn't have her cell with her. As unlikely as that was, it soothed him to think it.

Ending that effort when voice mail answered, he tried Abigail's number. Surely one of them would have a phone on her.

Two rings. A shrill voice said, "Hello?"

It took Reed a moment to realize he was talking to Dominic. What was that kid doing with Abigail's phone? Had he stolen it and taken off?

"Let me talk to Ms. Jones," Reed demanded.

"She's…" The boy fell silent, but the connection didn't. In the background Reed heard the sound of splintering wood. Someone screamed.

Lani yelled, "Stop. Police."

"Dominic!" Reed shouted into his phone.

"He broke the door!" the boy yelled.

Multiple voices rose in fright. Anger. Confusion. A puppy yipped.

And then there was the unmistakable sound of gunfire!

SEVENTEEN

Abigail dragged Dominic behind the sofa with her and kept him there as long as she could. It was a monumental struggle to hang on to the wiry teen.

Lani's voice came across strong. "He's down. Call 911!"

"I'll do it," the boy answered. With a twist and scramble he was out from behind the couch and had hold of Abigail's cell phone.

"It's not working," he reported. "Hello? Hello?"

Abigail took it from him and managed to calm herself enough to disconnect from the previous connection and report the break-in. She relayed the street address Lani called out to her and was assured that patrol units were on their way.

"Tell them it's an officer-involved shooting and we need an ambulance," Lani insisted. "I don't want them busting in here and taking me down by accident."

"Is he… Is he dead?" Abigail asked.

"Not yet. But he's not doing well," Lani replied.

No matter how nonchalant she sounded, Abigail could tell how deeply affected the other woman was because of the quaver in her voice and the fact that she'd backed up to a chair and sat while keeping her gun pointed at the wounded attacker.

"Who is he?" Lani asked.

Abigail shook her head. "I don't know. I've never seen him before. At least, I don't think I have." She glanced over at the teen. "Do you know him?"

The boy shook his head vigorously. "Uh-uh. No way."

By this time the injured man was moaning and holding his thigh. "I could have hit the femoral artery," Lani said. "We need to try to stop that bleeding or we could lose him."

"I'll do it," Abigail said. "Have you got a scarf or something like that handy?"

"Use a towel from the kitchen and his belt," Lani told her. "And be careful."

"Okay." As she cautiously approached the man she sensed Dominic at her elbow and told him to stay back.

"I can help. I can. Honest."

Rather than waste precious time arguing, Abigail opted to let him stay close. Truth to tell, she wasn't keen on nursing this person's leg, and the teen's presence was soothing her jangled nerves.

"Okay. You take his belt off while I apply pressure to the wound with the towel," she told him.

The job was done in a jiffy. Abigail sat back on her haunches. If her hands had been clean she would have high-fived the boy. Instead, she started to stand.

At that moment, the victim lunged. His shoulder rammed into her and sent her reeling. Dominic fell back, too, landing on his hands and feet like a crab.

Lani shouted, "Get out of the way!"

One thing was crystal clear to Abigail. Their so-called incapacitated victim was back on the move and dangerous. She threw herself to one side, hoping to get out of Lani's line of fire. Dominic, however, sprang up and made a grab for the man, spoiling the officer's aim.

"Dominic!" Abigail's heart was in her throat. If the rookie fired again she was sure to hit the boy by accident. "Stop! Stop!"

The limping, bleeding interloper used the door frame to scrape off the slightly built teen and leave him behind in a heap before making it all the way outside and disappearing.

Acting stunned, Dominic began to sob. Abigail fell to her knees beside him and gathered him up in her arms, mindless of the bloodstains.

She saw Lani run past, swing around the splintered door jamb and assume a shooter's stance.

Abigail was holding her breath, too shocked to move. As Lani's body relaxed and the firearm was lowered, she knew it was all over. They had probably just lost their best chance to identify one of her former attackers and she was thankful he had been the only one injured in the melee.

Yes, she was supposed to forgive her enemies, but she'd reserve that noble attempt for *after* he had been captured and jailed.

Lani tucked her gun into a holster, clipped it to her waist and went out onto the front porch to wait for the first responders.

"Don't let Midnight out," Abigail called after her.

Frowning, Lani stuck her head back inside. "Where is she, anyway?"

"The last time I saw her she was hiding behind the drapes," Abigail said. "I hope she's still there."

"She is," Lani answered. "Poor baby is terrified." She fastened a leash to the puppy's collar and gently coaxed her to come out. Even then, Midnight continued to tremble from nose to tail.

Busy comforting the boy, Abigail cast only a cursory glance at her pup. Lani was patiently consoling her. That would have to do until she and Dom could get cleaned up and take over. It was sad to see how frightened Midnight was.

Until she noticed Lani's frown, she didn't realize that the negative experience might have done damage to her impressionable Lab baby. Obviously Midnight was going to need a whole lot of cuddling and reassurance in the days and weeks to come.

Abigail was more than all right with that notion. She, herself, needed the same kind of TLC that the pup did. It was going to be good for both of them. After all, she had only her street kids and a few coworkers to count as family. There was nothing wrong with adding a furry member, as well.

Part of her mind wanted to include the Bransons, both of them. Lani had saved her life this time and Reed had rescued her in the past. But that was from her point of view. Theirs was the key. Reed had often insisted she was part of his job. And Lani? Well, the rookie cop couldn't be thrilled with them since she and Dominic had inadvertently let the attacker escape.

Abigail sighed and soaped her hands. It seemed as though trouble followed her wherever she went. And now, despite monumental efforts to help, she had involved both police officers as well as at least one of her homeless kids. That was unacceptable.

Then again, she thought, using a brush on her already clean fingernails, so was getting killed when she hadn't purposely done one thing wrong. Or had she? Could there be facts obscured by her lost memory that would paint a different picture?

Reed skidded his SUV to the curb between two patrol cars and ran into the house. If he'd seen the blood on the floor before spotting his loved ones he'd have shouted in anguish. Knowing it could have been theirs had things gone awry, he gathered up his sister and Abigail in a group hug.

"You, too, kid," he said, gesturing to Dominic. "I was listening to my radio on the way back and they said you tried to tackle the guy. Come here."

Hesitant to approach, Dom inched closer to the adults. "He got away."

"Thankfully," Reed said. "Look, I know you were doing what you thought was right, but it wasn't. Promise me you won't try anything like that again."

"Yeah, okay."

That simple agreement should have sufficed,

but Reed didn't like the intonation. Unless he was so overwrought he was imagining things, the teenager had his own agenda. That figured. After all, Dom was used to running wild and making his own decisions, the same as Kiera was.

Satisfied to hold Abigail and his sister however long they needed comforting, Reed found himself disappointed when they both eased away. In the background, one of the patrol officers was photographing the splintered door off the kitchen while a second inspected the backyard.

"I'll go get Jessie as soon as these officers are through," he said. "Where's the pup?"

"I put her in her crate in the bathroom to calm her down. She was a basket case after all this," Abigail said. "I didn't know what else to do and Lani said it would be best to give her some quiet time."

Reed nodded sagely. "That's fine. Where was she when the shooting started?"

"Hiding behind the sofa with me and Dominic," Abigail answered. "Lani was the only one who wasn't scared silly."

"Yeah, well," the other woman drawled. "I'm thankful I'd had the training to fall back on, but that doesn't mean I wasn't shaking."

"I'll talk to Noah Jameson and explain what

happened here. How you had no choice," Reed said. "I don't think it will hurt your chances for being assigned a working dog. Might slow things down a little, that's all."

Lani gestured to the uniformed officer who was inspecting the broken door. "He took my gun and bagged it."

"Standard operating procedure," Reed assured her.

She pulled a face. "I know, I know."

Reed turned to Abigail. "Could this guy have been the bigger one with the round cheeks? The one you couldn't really describe?"

"I don't think so, but it is possible. If I had heard him speak I might have a better idea. Everything happened so fast this time I can't be positive, but I don't remember anything he may have said."

"Okay. I'm sure our lab can get DNA from the blood he lost. It may take a while, though. They're always behind."

"How about fingerprints?"

"He was wearing gloves," the teen volunteered. "Didn't you see?"

"I guess I was too busy worrying he'd die before we got the bleeding stopped," Abigail answered. "I've had a first aid course for my job, but it didn't cover serious stuff like gunshots."

Reed looked askance. "Really? I'd think

that would be part of the normal curriculum. That and learning how to help victims of knife fights."

"Very funny," she said cynically. Reed could tell Abigail's nervousness was lessening. That was how this odd attitude worked for cops, fire-fighters and other first responders. They joked about the deathly serious aspects of their jobs as a tension reliever. The ones who never lightened up were bound to burn out a lot faster than their opposites did. Like what had happened to Abigail. The mind could take only so much trauma before it shut down.

Reed palmed his phone and thumbed through the photo albums before holding it up for her to see. "Take another look at the guy you were able to describe and try to picture him with the shooting victim."

Sighing, she seemed reluctant. Nevertheless, she stepped up and studied the face before closing her eyes. "Sorry. I'm not getting any flashes of insight. I really doubt they're connected, but if they aren't, then why come here and break down your door?"

"Good question." Reed was lowering his arm as the teenager inched closer. He raise the picture again. "What about you? Have you seen him down by the boardwalk or on the streets at Coney?"

Instead of offering a nonchalant no, Dominic began waving his hands and backing away. His dark eyes were wide and glistening. "No. No way. Never saw him before. Uh-uh."

Well, that was overkill. Reed stood still, observing the boy's reactions. He was lying. Big time. Not only had he seen the thin face Abigail had come up with, he knew who the man was and probably had a good idea where to find him. That was newsworthy. And troubling.

"Okay," Reed finally said, pocketing his phone when the boy hurried out of the room. "I'm going to find out how much longer these cops will be working our crime scene, then go get Jessie and put her in with Midnight to help calm her down. Later, I'll grab a hammer and repair the door frame. We can't leave it like that overnight."

"I'm really sorry," Abigail told him.

Reed checked to make certain Dominic was long gone before he leaned closer and said, "Don't always blame yourself, Abigail. What happened here today may have had little or nothing to do with you."

She began to frown and make a face. "Are you serious?"

"Serious as a gunshot to a leg," he said, deadpanning the quip. "There's something else going on and I plan to figure out what. Just go along with whatever I say or do, okay?"

"Sure." She shrugged. "Are you going to let your sister in on it, too?"

Casting a glance across the room at Lani and reading unspoken understanding in her expression, he said, "I doubt that will be necessary. She has the mind of a cop, same as I do. We're naturally suspicious of everybody and everything."

"I'm not sure I like that," Abigail admitted.

"Yeah, well, it beats looking at the world through rose-colored glasses and making yourself so vulnerable."

"Meaning me?"

"If the glasses fit." Reed could tell Abigail was upset. That was fine with him. If he could do or say anything that opened her eyes to the evil in their world and made her safer as a result, he would. It was a personal sacrifice to admit he didn't have a trusting nature because it showed him in a negative light. That could easily stop her from caring for him the way he cared for her. He could deal with that idea. He'd have to. But he didn't have to like it.

EIGHTEEN

Abigail spent the night tossing and turning, imagining all sorts of boogeymen hiding in the house or sneaking in and out through the windows the way the prowler had at her apartment. The old brick building in Brighton Beach had been noisier, but she'd been used to the ambient din of the busy city streets and her fellow tenants. Here, in Rego Park, it was so much quieter that every little noise stood out.

By morning she felt more weary than she had the evening before. Yawning, she joined Lani in the kitchen, drawn by the aroma of freshly brewed coffee. "Oh, that smells good."

The other woman filled a mug. "Here you go. Compliments of the cook."

Abigail chuckled, blew on the steaming liquid and took a cautious sip. "Mmmm. As good as it gets." She eyed Lani's jogging outfit. "Are you going running?"

"Been and back," Lani told her with a grin.

"You have to get up pretty early if you want to run with me. I walked your puppy, too. She's out in the yard now."

"Wow. I guess I need to set an alarm. I don't hit my stride until eight or so." She saluted with her mug. "And that's only after a couple shots of strong bean juice."

"Orange juice is better for you," Lani offered. "Want some?"

"No thanks." Abigail looked over her shoulder. "What about the guys? Any sign of Reed or Dom yet?"

"Nope. It's been nice and peaceful."

Laughing softly, Abigail nodded. "Believe me, I get it. I'm used to living alone."

"You don't get lonesome?"

"Sometimes." Another sip, another smile. "I am looking forward to having Midnight underfoot. She's a sweetheart. How was she acting this morning? Better?"

"Yes. I think she'll get over her fright from yesterday. If she'd been used to us and had developed more trust she'd have coped better. You have to remember, she hasn't been with you for very long. Socialization and bonding take time. You do realize you're only caretaking her, don't you?"

Sobering, Abigail nodded. "Yes, I know. How long can I expect her to stay with me?"

"As long as you participate in any formal training she may need, providing she improves enough to be considered for classes, you may be allowed to keep her at home for a year or two."

"That doesn't seem like very long at all." Abigail pictured those big brown eyes, velvety ears and feet almost the size of Jessie's, plopping against the floor like clown shoes. Midnight had just come into her life and she loved her already.

Reed's deep voice echoed down the hallway. "Dominic?"

Abigail swiveled to greet him as he entered. "Good morning."

"Where's Dominic?"

She and Lani shrugged. "We thought you were both sleeping in."

Instead of explaining, Reed stomped to the front door and jerked it open, then slammed it and circled through the kitchen to the rear. The patched door stuck slightly, but he strong-armed it open long enough to call, "Dominic!" without letting the eager dogs in.

"I didn't see him when I put the puppy out with Jessie," Lani said. "Wasn't he on the cot we fixed for him?"

"No. I thought maybe he'd moved in here to the sofa, but I can see he didn't." Raking his fingers through his short, dark hair, Reed began to pace. "We had a good man-to-man talk last night, and I assumed he understood that I wanted to be his friend and help him. Considering the rough life he's had, I should have guessed he'd take off instead of trusting me."

That conclusion settled in Abigail's stomach like a rock. "You think he's left?"

"Absolutely."

"Why? He knows he's safer here with us."

"Is he?" Reed strapped on his utility belt and opened the combination lock on the gun safe where he stored his duty weapon. "Tell me," he said, directing the query to Abigail, "when you said he was trying to stop the guy Lani shot, is it possible he was trying to leave with him instead?"

"No, I..." She reran the chaotic scene in her mind. Reed had a point. "I suppose he could have been. I just assumed, since he'd been helping me with first aid, that he was on my side. Our side. What makes you think he was trying to escape?"

"The way he reacted to the reconstruction of the face of your assailant. My mistake was thinking he was more afraid of that man than he was of staying here with us."

Reed's sister asked, "Do you want me to call it in as a missing person?"

"Not yet. I need to report to Noah Jameson before I do anything else. He left the decision up to me, and I'm the one who made the mistake of bringing Dom home. If Abigail hadn't been with us I probably wouldn't have. Let's assume the boy headed back to the beach and go there first."

"Are you going to put Jessie on his trail?" Lani asked.

It was clear to Abigail that her presence was posing a problem when both Bransons turned to stare at her. "I can stay here with Midnight if you need to go," she said.

"No good. Lani's trained in self-defense, but you aren't. The police still have her gun, and that puppy won't be any help. We'll all have to go."

"Even Midnight?"

"No. Lani can crate her for the short time we'll be away so she won't slow us down. I'll let Jessie track Dom as far as she can, then turn her over to you two and you can bring her back here—hopefully with a police escort—and wait for me. He's a savvy kid. He'll probably hop on the subway. Once he boards a train, Jessie's bound to lose his trail."

As far as Abigail was concerned, his plan was awful. However, this was not the time to argue. The sooner they put the bloodhound on the teen's trail, the better. When it came time to leave Reed and come back to the house with Lani, she'd speak her piece. No way was she letting that stubborn cop track down one of her special kids without her. Period.

Besides, she reasoned, she'd feel a lot safer with Reed by her side than she would if they parted. She might not be used to his house yet, but she was more than used to being with him. He was the glue that held her psyche together and the strength that gave her enough courage to keep trying.

That, and my faith in God, Abigail added. Lately it seemed she only remembered to pray earnestly when she was scared to death, so her next prayer was an apology to her heavenly Father and the promise to do better at trusting Him in all things, even the smallest detail.

Starting now, she told herself, giving thanks for Reed even if he was an opinionated, stubborn man who drove her crazy.

Reed felt overwhelmed and he was not happy about it. He couldn't report the boy when all he had was a suspicion. It was going to be hard enough getting somebody to look after Abigail when Lani had to go back to work and he sure couldn't divert the talents of his extraordinary K-9, he added. Jessie had found a trail the instant she'd hit the back door. Nose down, she was coursing back and forth, rarely lifting her head to sniff the air.

Reed glanced over his shoulder at the women. Lani was dressed for running but Abigail was going to get overheated in those jeans and that long-sleeve T-shirt. She was already wiping her brow.

"I can't stop now," he called back. "If you can't keep up, head back to the house."

A breathless, "No way," drifted back to him. He should have guessed Abigail would stick it out until he ended the search or she dropped from exhaustion. She was the most stubborn— and loyal—woman he'd ever encountered, with the possible exception of his overachieving sister. Lani had always insisted she was as capable as he was, and now she'd met her doppelganger in Abigail Jones.

Streets grew busier and traffic thick. Trucks honked. Taxis squeezed in and out between other vehicles as if able to flex as they passed, much the way a terrier pursued a rabbit through brambles or down its burrow.

Jessie halted, circled once, then started down the stairway into the first subway entrance they came to.

"This is it," Reed announced. "As I suspected, he hopped a train."

Lani accepted Jessie's leash from him. "You really want us to go back home? Why don't you come along and get your car?"

"It'll take too long," he countered. "I'll contact Transit and make arrangements for them to keep an eye out, particularly near the Coney and Brighton stops."

"Okay," his sister said.

Pulling out his phone Reed covered the opposite ear with his hand to mute the street noise and turned away.

It took several minutes to complete his explanation and give the dispatcher a detailed description of Dominic. Since the boy owned so few clothes it was easy to tell what he had to be wearing. When Reed looked behind him, expecting to see Lani, Jessie and Abigail on their way back to his house, he was stunned. His sister and his dog were gone, all right. But Abigail Jones was still standing there, grinning up at him as if she had just won a prize.

"What are you doing here? And where's Lani? You're supposed to stay with her."

"I decided to stick with you, instead. Your sister didn't seem to mind." Abigail pointed back the way they had come. "She said she was taking Jessie home."

"Well, *I* do." He shaded his eyes to scan the busy sidewalk. There was no sign of Lani's blond hair, and Jessie was too close to the ground to spot at a distance, given the throng of pedestrians.

"Sorry," Abigail said, continuing to smile. "Too late. I'm going to be there for that kid, even if he is trouble with a capital *T*. You're stuck with me until we catch up to Dom."

Gritting his teeth and clamping his jaw, he stared at her. So pretty. So witty. And so, so…

She gestured at the descending staircase and the crush of passengers zigzagging past each other. "Are we going to stand here arguing or get a move on? I'm sure Dominic didn't waste any time."

Reed did the only logical thing. He clasped her hand tightly and started down the stairs, half dragging her behind him. There were no words adequate for this situation. None. Not even the unacceptable ones she had hinted at.

Right here, right now, all he could do was make sure she didn't lag behind or pull some other inane trick that made matters even worse. If that was possible.

He felt her resist. Heard her say, "There. That one. It's the most direct route."

She was breathless and softly laughing. He was not amused.

"You don't have to worry about me trying to ditch you," she said, raising her voice to carry above the rhythmic clacking of the wheels on the tracks. "I told you. I intend to be there for

Dom. The way I see it, you're my best chance of catching up to him."

Leaning closer, he spoke into her ear, his warm breath tickling her cheek and sending a shiver from there to the ends of every nerve.

"I'd be more inclined to trust you," Reed said, "if you kept your word."

She whipped around as best she could without staggering. "Hey, when have I lied to you?" Abigail wasn't sorry she'd used a harsh tone, but she sure wished she hadn't placed her face so close to his while doing it. Their lips were mere inches apart, and unless Reed straightened there was no chance she was going to be able to back away. The accidental closeness was overwhelming. Awesome. It was as if they were the only two people on that train, enclosed in a cocoon of intense awareness and emotional pull. Connected as never before.

To her delight, Reed seemed as stunned as she felt. Frozen in time, he stared into her eyes, studying, probing their depths, asking unspoken questions she didn't dare answer.

A little notion formed and grew beyond her wildest imagining. If the train jerked just a tiny bit and she let herself go with it, there was a chance Reed would feel the same urge she did and kiss her. They'd had their differences, sure, but the attraction felt mutual. It simply had to be.

There was no way she'd have become so enamored of him if she hadn't sensed reciprocation.

When had it started? she wondered. How had she managed to meet and fall for this man in such a short time? Was she deluded? Unbalanced because of the amnesia?

Amnesia. Abigail closed her eyes and stood stock-still, her face still raised to his. She was seeing the carousel, the night, the men who had been nothing but shimmering shadows until she'd worked through the problem with Danielle and come up with a face.

She was in Luna Park. Alone. Frightened. And she was watching two adults manhandle a smaller person, probably a teen or preteen. Then they were after her. Someone grabbed her. Threatened her. Hurt her wrists and made her believe she was about to be murdered!

Abigail's lips parted. Her breathing grew ragged. She remembered!

Her eyes flew open just as Reed was lowering his mouth to join it with hers and her noisy gasp ended everything.

She had no time to lament the show of affection she'd missed by moments. This was too exciting. She grabbed his arm. "I know what I saw! It's all clear now."

"You remembered the whole event? Really?"

"Yes! It was—it was by the carousel. Two

men, one heavy and one thinner, just like I told you before. Only now I know why they chased and grabbed me. I saw them restraining a third person. I think it was one of my kids. It had to be. Who else would be hanging around down there at that hour? Besides…"

More details swam to the surface, giving Abigail a jolt. "Hey! I know why I was there. It was because of Kiera. She'd asked me to meet her."

"No wonder she was so nervous about your memories. She was involved. Do you think she set you up?"

Abigail's spirits plummeted from the mountaintop of success to the valley of despair. "I don't know. I'd like to think she wouldn't do that to me but I can't be positive, especially after the way she made Dominic run away from us."

To her relief, Reed slipped an arm around her and held her close to his side while they swayed with the movement of the train. "One answer at a time," he said. "First we'll find him, then we'll look for her. If we have to round up every kid on the boardwalk, we will."

"Can you do that?"

He huffed. "Not out of uniform like this. But I do think I can get the acting chief of my unit to pull a few strings. We've had reports of a couple of newly missing teens anyway, so it's not a stretch to do a sweep."

"*My* kids? Why didn't you tell me?"

"Simmer down. These kids were visiting from out of town and disappeared during a day at the beach with friends."

"That is so sad." She leaned against Reed for support and to draw on his inner strength. "Sometimes I feel as though my best efforts are worthless. I can't rescue all the lost kids no matter how hard I try."

"Then you understand how I feel," he said with a sigh. "Only in your case, some of them actually come to you. I have to chase them down or try to outsmart them. A lot of times, my collars will make bail or alibi out and hit the streets again before I have time to grab lunch."

"I sometimes wish I could lock these kids up and force them to listen to good advice," Abigail said.

He gave her a tender squeeze. "And I wish my contacts liked me half as much as yours like you."

"*I* like you," she told him.

"Yeah," Reed said. She felt his voice rumbling in his chest where her cheek rested. "Don't tell anybody, but I kinda like you, too, Ms. Jones."

NINETEEN

"We could cover more ground if we split up," Abigail said.

Reed scowled at her. "You have to be kidding." It was a relief to see her blush behind those freckles.

"I thought I should at least suggest it."

"No. Period. You and I are doing this together or not at all. Got that?"

She squeezed his hand. "Yup. Got it."

"You're agreeing with me? What's wrong? Are you sick? Running a fever?"

"Ha ha." She held up one hand and placed the tips of her index finger and thumb less than an inch apart. "I don't want to get even this far away from you, okay?"

"That works for me." Reed couldn't help smiling. When he saw her sky blue eyes sparkling he almost embraced her again. If he could have come up with a good reason to, he would have.

"Since you're down here all the time and I'm not, why don't you choose where we look first?"

"Now you're the one who's acting strange," Abigail said with a wry smile. "But I get it. I do know where the kids like to hang out, although this is pretty early to catch any of them awake. They stay up late and sleep late."

"Where? Where do they sleep?"

She shrugged. "A lot of them stay on the beach in warm weather. That'll be ending soon, and it worries me. Come on."

Reed followed her down a ramp that led to the sand. It was too loose for comfortable walking, but he persevered. Sky that had been clear blue with a few puffy clouds was now darkening noticeably. "We should have brought jackets."

"Yes. I never dreamed it would turn so chilly in September."

"It's hard to imagine anybody spending the winter here, let alone a bunch of kids. That's a recipe for trouble."

"Don't I know it." Abigail shivered. "Most of them go into the city center when it gets too bad down here. A few come to us for aid and shelter. Those are the ones I look forward to seeing because it means they're ready to listen to reason. The state, as well as my organization, AFS, have plenty of programs to get them jobs or schooling or whatever they need. But they have to be willing to follow a few simple rules and that's where we sometimes run into conflict."

"I'm sure you do."

Just ahead, near the water's edge, a flock of gulls took flight and scattered, screeching in protest. Reed thought he'd seen something hit the beach near them so he wasn't too surprised they'd panicked. He did, however, inspect the wet sand where he'd seen the disturbance and he didn't like the narrow groove he spotted.

"What's that from?"

"My guess? A bullet trajectory." He began to scoop with his hands until he turned up a piece of lead-colored metal.

"That's impossible. I didn't hear any big bang."

"You wouldn't be likely to recognize the sound from this small a caliber. It would be like listening to plinking at a shooting gallery." Placing himself as a human shield between the boardwalk and the young woman, Reed scanned inland. All looked peaceful. A few folks were sweeping spots in front of food stands, and carts were delivering supplies for the upcoming day, but other than normal activity, there was nothing going on. If there had been a shooter he was either hiding or had left after firing the warning shot.

"Okay," Reed said, "we're getting off this

sand and back to where we can take up defensive positions if we have to."

"But the kids…"

"Come on. We'll find a seat close to Kiera's favorite hot dog stand, watch and wait. If Dominic is around he may go there looking for her. Being in a crowd is smarter than wandering around like a row of lone ducks in a shooting gallery."

"So much for letting me take the lead," she muttered as they crossed the sand again.

"It's not your fault." He held up the tiny bullet. "I just have an aversion to ending up with one of these in me."

"I'd hate it, too."

"That's comforting." Reed told her.

Staying alert, he continued to scan the quiet stretches of boardwalk on either side of them while choosing chairs that backed up to an enormous menu sign. If the shooter was hiding, he or she would have to step into view to get a bead on them, giving Reed a chance to mount an effective defense.

The sigh Abigail loosed was almost as noisy as the wind off the Atlantic. Reed saw her shiver. "Cold?"

"A little. We left in too big a hurry to plan well."

"I know." He made a face of disgust. "My

fault. Waking up and not finding Dominic rattled me. That's unacceptable for a cop. I know better."

"Yeah, well, when you care about somebody your emotions can take charge of your brain." She chuckled wryly. "I should know. I'm down here with you, just as unprepared."

He patted the concealed holster at his waist. "I'm not exactly unprepared. Underprepared is more like it." He glanced at the gray sky. "Once the sun comes out it'll warm up so much we'll be complaining of the heat."

"I suppose." Abigail had been fidgeting. She stood. "I can't just sit here, okay?"

Reaching out, Reed stopped her by touching her arm. "Wait. Look." He pointed as surreptitiously as he could. "Isn't that the girl?"

Abigail twisted around, squinted. "Yes!"

"Easy. It looks like she's coming to us. Let her."

"You're right."

As Reed watched, the teenager spotted them and broke into a run. She was approaching so fast he expected to see a pursuer. There was none. The boardwalk behind her was empty.

Abigail opened her arms and the girl collapsed into the embrace. She was weeping. Gasping. Trying to speak.

"He got me out…" Sobs interrupted.

"Who did?" Reed asked.

"D-Dominic. He was supposed to be right behind me, but he didn't make it!"

"Okay, slow down and explain," Reed said. All the response he got was more weeping, so he turned the job over to Abigail. "Get her calmed down. We need details."

"Right." Abigail shepherded the teen to the chairs she and Reed had been sharing. "Here. Sit with me and take some deep breaths. We need to know what happened. Where's Dominic?"

"*They* have him," Kiera blurted. "And they're going to put him on a ship." A gasp. "Today!"

"A ship? Why?" Abigail asked.

Speaking louder to be heard above the gut-wrenching sobs, Reed was hoping against hope that he was wrong. "How many kids do they have?"

"L-lots," Kiera blubbered.

"All young and mostly girls?"

The frantic teen nodded.

"Can you lead us back there?"

"I—I can't go back. If they catch me they'll kill me."

The puzzled expression on Abigail's face told Reed she was not yet seeing the whole picture, so he explained. "Human trafficking. We've suspected as much for months but haven't been able to gather enough evidence to make arrests.

This could be the breakthrough we've all been praying for."

He pulled out his cell phone to report to his boss and saw light dawning in Abigail's eyes. Awareness was rapidly replaced by anger and determination.

She grasped Kiera's shoulders and forced a face-to-face confrontation. "Listen to me. This is what's going to happen. You are going to tell the police what you know and where the prisoners are being held. And then, if they have trouble finding the hiding place, you and I are going to lead them there. Understood?"

"Noooo!"

"Oh, yes. Somebody has to stand up for these other kids. Dominic risked his life to free you. Can you do less for him?"

Reed stayed out of it. He watched the girl sink to her knees, then saw Abigail lift her back up. They both had to be scared to death, particularly since both had been victims of similar attacks. It was only by the grace of God that Abigail had managed to outwit her pursuers and develop into a valuable ally.

He could not have been prouder of her if she had been his sister or a fellow police officer. All he had to worry about now was keeping her in the background while the NYPD handled the assault on the kidnappers' stronghold and freed their prisoners.

He huffed. That should be about as easy as turning the tide at will.

The best he could do was shoot a prayer toward Heaven and leave it to God, because no way was Abigail Jones going to listen to any other warning.

One element of the morning's operation was driving Abigail crazy. She hated waiting. However, she was also smart enough to realize that a Lone Ranger approach was foolhardy.

As patrol car after patrol car rolled up to the staging area along Surf Avenue and angled into the curb, she was astounded at the number of regular officers, SWAT team members and K-9s with their partners.

The only person she recognized for sure was Brianne, the one who had delivered the replacement SUV to Reed after his was wrecked. All business, the K-9 officer was accompanied by a golden Lab who looked more mature than the second dog of the same color who trotted along beside a male officer.

After shaking hands with many of the assembled police, Reed stepped back to listen to their incident commander issue instructions. As soon as assignments had been parceled out, Reed returned to Abigail, accompanied by the others with K-9s.

"Brianne Hayes you know," he said. "This is Stella, Midnight's mother. She's a former patrol K-9 being cross-trained at present."

Abigail nodded. Her arm remained firmly around Kiera's waist so the teen couldn't flee. "Yes. Hello again."

"And this is Finn Gallagher with K-9 Abernathy. His specialty is search and rescue. I hope we won't need either dog today."

"So do I." Abigail managed a slight smile for the others and their amazing canines. "I'm Abigail Jones and this is Kiera Underhill. She managed to escape from kidnappers this morning and is going to lead us to their hideout, if necessary." She gave the teen a squeeze. "Aren't you?"

"I guess." The face Kiera made to accompany her response was anything but amiable. Abigail didn't care. She couldn't let anything stop the rescue. There were some things that took precedence over the sentiments of a pouting, sniffling, uncooperative adolescent, and this was one of them.

"We saw your sister arrive in your car," Brianne said to Reed. "She's got your dog and your uniform with her."

"Great!" Reed looked directly at Abigail.

"Stay put. I'll go get Jessie and my gear and be right back."

Left with the other K-9 officers and their dogs, Abigail felt out of place. Nevertheless, she held her ground.

"I really admire what you all do," she told them. "I had no idea how complicated your job is or how hard you train to keep your dogs working well."

Brianne smiled down at the yellow Lab at her side. "Stella got off to a kind of slow start when she arrived from the Czech Republic. She was the gift that kept giving."

"You mean her puppies?"

Brianne's smile grew to a grin. "Yes. They're adorable, of course, but she couldn't work when we first got her and I don't speak her language so she had to relearn everything in English. If it had been German, one of our bilingual trainers could have taken over, but there's too much difference in the commands in Czech."

"It's probably harder for her than it is for us," Abigail guessed.

"I'm not sure of that. She's really smart." Fondness in the female officer's expression made it clear that she truly admired and loved Stella despite the obstacles they'd had to overcome.

"I hope Midnight takes after her," Abigail

said. "She's so adorable. I'd love to see her succeed at something, even if she doesn't have what
it takes to be a police dog."

"Don't feel bad. They don't all make the cut,"
Brianne said. "At least one pup from her litter
has already washed out."

"How disappointing. Maybe they can become
service or therapy dogs."

The officer was nodding. "Maybe. We only
accept the best of the best in the NYPD."

"Dogs, you mean?" Abigail felt her cheeks
warming.

"And men and women," Brianne replied, obviously enjoying the brief moment of shared
amusement. "Reed Branson is one of the best."
She paused before adding, "In and out of uniform."

"Are you and he…? I mean is he…? Oh, never
mind."

Brianne laughed. "Relax, I do have someone
special who used to be in the K-9 unit. Gavin
Sutherland and I are engaged."

"I'm happy for you."

"I imagine there are personal reasons you're
glad it's not Branson," Brianne teased. "Head's
up. Here he comes. He's all yours."

In the background, Finn gave a cynical
chuckle. "Better not let him hear you giving
him away like a lost pup."

Abigail had been so enthralled by her conversation with the other K-9 officer, she'd forgotten that they weren't alone. The blush she'd sensed before probably developed into a crimson that washed out her freckles and clashed with her red hair.

To distract herself, she scanned the distant beach in the direction opposite of where the cops were gathering. All breath left her. She froze, barely able to speak. Finally, she managed to point with her free hand and say, "Look! Way over there by the steps. Are those the guys you're looking for? One is limping. Maybe he's the guy that was shot."

Everyone within hearing distance swiveled and stared, including Reed. "I can't tell exactly what you're seeing but I'm going to find out." He grabbed his radio and broadcast the possible sighting. The pair had already reached and were crossing the boardwalk.

Shouting, "Stay here," Reed took off at a run rather than wait for backup and lose sight of his quarry.

Worried, excited and acting on impulse, Abigail thrust Kiera at Brianne and yelled, "Watch her," as a surge of adrenaline overpowered her usual common sense and convinced her to follow.

Struggling across the soft beach, she made

a dash for the closest stairway leading up from the sand. This was her territory, the place where she'd felt most at home until she'd been attacked.

Once on solid footing, she didn't join the rush of police officers heading for Reed's last known position. Instead, she managed to stay parallel with him and Jessie, arriving at the junction of a street and an alley behind some concessions just as the other pursuers appeared down the block to her right.

Abigail felt like cheering until she noticed she was about to come face to face with the thugs they'd been after. "Oh, no!"

The two miscreants skidded to a stop and one pointed a gun at her. The thin-faced weasel was supporting his limping companion. That man fit the build of her second attacker. When he stared at her and said, "I should have killed you when I had the chance," she was positive it was him. The hair on her arms prickled. Her mouth was suddenly so dry she couldn't swallow, couldn't speak, couldn't move a muscle.

The larger man shook off his partner and faced her. She saw his eyes begin to squint. He pointed the muzzle of his gun at her, ignoring an ever growing cadre of armed police officers approaching with caution.

Abigail didn't know what to do so she simply stood there. Men were shouting over each other in the background, their individual commands lost in the din.

She saw her nemesis start to sneer, acting as if he didn't realize or didn't care that he was so greatly outnumbered. Then, something moved directly behind him. It was Reed!

Reed made a grab for the man's gun and missed. It fired, sending a bullet whizzing past Abigail's ear. She screamed.

An instinct for survival propelled her backward. She staggered. The gun came to bear on her once more. Was this the end? The part of her that knew she loved Reed kept insisting that her life could not end until she had told him how she felt.

She squeezed her eyes closed and covered her face with her hands, waiting for a second shot. Unidentified hands grabbed her roughly and lifted while fingers pressed tightly at her throat, choking the breath out of her. She was helpless. Finished.

Beautiful, colorful lights flashed behind her eyelids. Overwhelmed and overburdened she accepted the version of reality that was commanding her imagination and sank into oblivion.

TWENTY

Reed saw what was happening and roared with primal rage. He launched himself, landing on the back of the thug who was choking Abigail. One arm tightened around the front of the man's neck, elbow bent, and he completed the choke hold by grasping his own wrist for leverage.

Released, Abigail dropped limply into the arms of other officers who lowered her gently to the ground. Reed's anger consumed him, and he tightened his hold despite orders to let go. If not for Abigail's soft moan breaking through the haze of roiling emotion he might have continued indefinitely.

Reed picked out her moan above the sounds of traffic, the grunts and curses of his adversary and a multitude of police officers all shouting at the same time.

Abigail! She was still alive.

Reed pushed the burly kidnapper toward a nearby group of patrolmen. Abigail's eyelids were fluttering. He gathered her in his arms and began to rock back and forth.

"Wake up. Please, wake up." Gently kissing her hand, he prayed with an intensity of pure faith that surprised him. "Please, Jesus. Please send her back to me."

Blue eyes opened and looked up. Thankful beyond words, Reed forgot his macho image. It was just them. Him and his Abigail. Together. "Thank You, Jesus."

Unashamed, he let the tears roll down his cheeks to mingle with hers in the instant before he pulled her to him and repeated his heavenly thanks over and over.

Abigail clung to him. Her breathing was raspy, her slim body shuddering as she struggled to take in enough air.

Finally, she whispered a weak, "Amen."

That was good enough for Reed. More of his tears dampened her silky red hair and his shoulders shook.

As others began to arrive and he was forced to pull himself together, Jessie pushed through and began to lick the salty drops off his cheeks.

It would have suited Abigail better if neither she nor Reed had been required to submit to a medical checkup. She kept repeating, "I'm fine. See? Standing up and breathing," which was punctuated part of the time by a croupy cough that negated what she was saying.

With her at the rear of the waiting ambulance, Reed was watching closely. Abigail was thankful he hadn't been hurt and felt terrible that she'd put everyone in more jeopardy because she'd gotten involved when she should have stayed back. She would have apologized ad infinitum if Reed's scowl hadn't stopped her.

Brianne had already reported that one of the two men they'd grappled with was in custody. The other had slipped away and escaped while everyone's attention was focused on Reed and the man trying to strangle Abigail.

Finn and Brianne showed up at the ambulance to deliver news of the latest developments. Wisely, Abigail kept silent as they briefed Reed.

"Danielle is putting a trace on the calls made from the big guy's cell," Brianne said. "As soon as we get solid info we'll mount a strike against the rest of the gang. In the meantime, precinct cops raided the place where the girl said she'd been held."

"Let me guess," Reed said, wincing when he moved. "It was empty."

"Unfortunately," Finn answered. "We're checking street view cameras to see if we can get a lead. If that teenager is right and they plan to ship out a load of trafficked kids tonight, it will probably be at high tide, meaning we have until 10:00 p.m. to locate them."

Although Abigail was listening, her mind was also spinning. If she were the kidnappers, where would she hide prisoners? They'd probably want to stick close to the shore or a harbor even though patrols would be thick now that the authorities knew what was going down. Those poor, poor kids must be so scared. And unless Kiera had lied, Dominic Walenski was still among them. So where could they be?

There were a couple of abandoned warehouses in Brighton Beach that came to mind. Abigail knew that kind of place was a favorite of homeless kids, especially once the weather worsened. Those buildings also would provide a fertile hunting ground if the kidnap ring was short of victims.

She cast a surreptitious glance at Reed. He was straightening his uniform, clearly intending to continue to assist with the ongoing search. If she was going to divert him, now was the perfect time.

Waiting until he looked ready, Abigail gently touched his shoulder. "Please, don't go."

"I have to."

"But…" She looped her hand through his arm and urged him to step aside. "I have an idea."

"Uh-oh. The last time you had an idea we got shot at."

Not about to be deterred, she tried another approach. "I think I may know where the kidnap ring stashed those kids."

"What took you so long to say so?"

"I didn't say I was positive. I just have an idea. What will it hurt to go with me and see? You'll hear about any new leads over the radio in your car wherever you are."

"I gather you want me to drive you somewhere?"

"Not just anywhere. To a couple of places where homeless kids tend to gather in the winter. What can it hurt?"

"My job," Reed quipped. "I'd like to keep it."

Abigail ignored his cynicism. "We won't be going far. You'll be close by if and when these other officers nail down a location." She pulled a face and directed it at the bevy of squad cars along the street. "Personally, I think it would be a lot smarter to try to sneak up on these traffickers. Look at all those cops. You'd think they were going after the mafia."

"This is organized crime, whether it's a worldwide organization or a hometown operation," Reed said. "Chances are, unless these kids get sick and die on the voyage, they'll be sold to the highest bidder. Think about it. They leave home looking for freedom and end up a prisoner in the worst kind of jail."

The weight of his words settled in her heart and left a bleeding wound that might never heal unless they rescued the helpless young teens. Then she spied something in his expression that she could only hope she understood.

"You're going to take me, aren't you?"

Reed gave her a cynical look and shook his head as if disgusted with himself, not her. When he said, "Yes, God help me," Abigail couldn't hold back a grin. Okay, they might not be successful. Other searchers might have better results. But that wasn't the takeaway here. Reed was *trusting* her. *Completely.* She felt like cheering, and would have, if she wasn't afraid of triggering another coughing fit.

Jessie trotted along beside Reed, tail waving like a flag, nose up, testing the air. On his opposite side, Abigail felt as much elation as the K-9 was demonstrating. Only Reed, bracketed between them, seemed morose.

It wasn't until they were back in his car and halfway to Brighton Beach that his mood lifted. A radio call was asking their location in relation to the block of empty warehouses she had already pinpointed.

Abigail was ecstatic. "That's it!" she shouted across the car. "That's where we're headed. And we'll get there a good ten minutes faster because we have a head start."

Reed radioed their position, then glanced over at her, his eyebrows raised. "How did you figure that out?"

"Logic," she said, pointing to her temple, "and brains."

"Ha!" For the first time since that morning, she heard him start to laugh. Really laugh. From her crate in the rear, Jessie joined in with a howl.

Abigail would have enjoyed the moment a lot more if Reed's laugh hadn't sounded so sarcastic.

Pulling up a block short of the designated warehouse, Reed parked in an alley and got out.

As he released his K-9, he gave Abigail a stern glare. "You are not going."

"Yes, I am. I've been inside before. You need me."

"Only if I want to complicate everything," he countered. "This time somebody might aim at me instead of you."

"Have I mentioned lately how sorry I am for getting in your way?"

"Yes, you have. That doesn't mean I'm ready to make you my partner. Jessie is all I need." With that, he started off, assuming she'd stay behind.

When she hustled to keep up with him, instead, he halted. "Go. Back. To. The. Car."

"I don't think so."

"Aargh!" Pausing for a deep, calming breath, he regained his composure. Faced her. Said, "Ms. Jones, you are the most obstinate person, man or woman, I have ever met. However, if you're half as intelligent as you claim to be, you'll realize that you're putting everyone in more danger by insisting on sticking with me. Stop and think for a second. Please."

That did it. Reed saw the fire leave her blue eyes and watched her shoulders sag. She finally got the picture. With a barely discernible nod, Abigail returned to the SUV, fished around in the passenger seat and emerged holding Dominic's satin jacket.

"You may need this," she said calmly. "I noticed he'd left it in the car after he worked with your tech person."

"Perfect. Thanks." A tense moment came and went. "Well?"

She pulled out her cell and waved it. "If you need me, call. I'll be right here."

"Good." Wondering how long her promise was going to last, Reed silenced his radio and left her. Circling the old brick warehouse, he turned the corner to the loading dock in the rear and glanced back. No Abigail. What a relief.

He understood why she was so bent on being in on the capture. She loved those mixed-up kids. Identified with them, according to what she'd told him about her past. But that didn't mean it was smart for her to get underfoot when a police operation was in play.

Once the other units arrived and they had the building surrounded, he'd be ready to show Jessie the jacket and give her the command to seek. Entry was bound to be chaotic. When he located Dom, however, chances were good that the other kidnapped kids would be close by.

Jessie heard the noise first and froze, fully alert. Reed stiffened. Followed the dog's cues and stared at the roll-up door above the concrete loading platform. Chains rattled. Muted voices drifted out through the corrugated metal portal.

The door began to rise.

Reed fell back, taking Jessie with him and giving her the signal for silence. The only close hiding place was behind a large trash bin, so he hunkered down there to watch.

A box truck like the one that had smashed into his first SUV was rattling up the street behind the warehouse and turning in to the drive. One headlight was shattered, its chrome frame flapping. The front bumper was canted, too. He didn't need forensics to decide this had to be the same vehicle that had been aimed at Abigail.

Anger rose. He tamped it down. Emotional responses were self-defeating. What he needed was to radio his position and report on the developments before the kidnap ring loaded the truck and it sped off crammed with victims.

He keyed his mic. Static echoed in his earpiece. "On scene, ten-ten. This is a ten-thirteen. Repeat, officer needs assistance."

A garbled reply told him little. Either the Dumpster was heavy enough to interfere with radio transmissions or dispatch had more than one incident working at once. The latter was most likely. After all, this was New York City, even if this particular raid was taking place on the fringes.

The truck made a three-point turn and stopped, its rear to the dock. The driver was new to him, but he recognized Abigail's remaining original assailant as the passenger. This was the right place for sure. So where was his backup?

Reed looked down at Jessie with affection. She hadn't been trained for anything but tracking, so he wasn't going to put her life in danger by taking her with him if he was forced to act alone. That would not have been his choice. Not in the slightest. But he couldn't just stand by and watch a bunch of kids loaded into a truck that would take them somewhere so terrible it was almost beyond imagining.

I still have a little time, Reed told himself. *It's only a matter of minutes until backup arrives.*

Did he have minutes? He thought so, hoped so.

Someone inside the dark warehouse started to wail. The sound of a slap echoed out the open bay door and the noise ceased immediately.

Shadows began to fill the portal. Myriad feet shuffled forward. The victims were chained together at the ankles. They could walk but there was no chance any of them could run, even if Reed somehow managed to distract their captors.

He heard sirens in the distance. So did the kidnappers. One of the guards prodded the group of abused teens forward with a rifle. "Faster or I'll shoot you where you stand."

Reed was about to show himself in a last-ditch effort to prevent the thugs from loading their prisoners when he heard a familiar voice coming from across the dock.

"You won't shoot anybody," Abigail shouted. "If you do, nobody will be able to move a step because they'll be dragging dead weight."

Where was she? Reed couldn't tell. Thankfully, her common sense warning seemed to have gotten through to the armed men. One called to the other. "See, dummy? I told you it was stupid to tie 'em all together like that."

"Well how was I to know? I didn't wanna lose any more."

Multiple sirens overlapped each other. The cacophony grew. A patrol car skidded across the driveway to Reed's left, blocking the truck's escape. Officers piled out, crouching down and running for cover.

The man with the rifle turned and fired at the car.

Reed shouted, "Everybody down!" at the frightened teens.

To his horror he saw that Abigail had joined the group of victims and was trying to drag them, en masse, back into the warehouse. Her task was a jumble of legs and arms and toppling bodies.

Gunfire continued from the thugs while cops circled the building, taking care to not aim at the teens.

One of the criminals chose a human shield and appeared at the door, illuminated by police floodlights.

Reed was both shocked and terrified.

The man had grabbed the only civilian who wasn't chained. Abigail Jones.

Abigail was not about to become a victim again. She hadn't had time to learn much about self-defense from Lani but she had seen one move that might work. Cupping her fist in her opposite hand she drove her elbow into the man's stomach as hard as she could. He gasped, released her and folded like a limp rag. She threw herself to the side.

Recovering quickly, the rifleman straightened and pointed his weapon at the prisoners. Abigail cringed next to Dominic and held him close. There was no way for her to shield all the captive teens. If this was the end, then so be it. She'd done all she possibly could.

A volley of shots echoed.

A kidnapper threatening them collapsed. The weasel-looking guy from the truck and its driver immediately raised their hands. Weasel screeched, "Don't shoot! I give up."

In seconds the officers closed in and it was over. Abigail hugged the teen she'd grown so fond of. "Dom. Are you okay?"

The only reply she got was a tightening of his hug and shaking of his shoulders. She stroked his dark hair.

Reed soon joined them. Abigail was delighted that he included them both in his embrace and she clung to him, unashamed, unafraid. It might take weeks to sort out all the crimes this gang had committed but that was inconsequential measured against the astounding rescue. She didn't even care if she got a royal chewing out from every cop in New York. Saving those kids had been worth the risk. If she hadn't physically forced them to move, to try to get themselves out of the line of fire, there was no telling how many would have, could have, been wounded. Or worse. That horrible thought made her weak in the knees.

Reed's breath was ragged against her hair. When he kissed the top of her head she thought she heard him swallow a sob. Tears filled her eyes. Relief filled her heart and mind. The nightmare was over. Her memory was restored. The threat had been eliminated and lives had been saved. It was possible her joy-filled dreams could now unfold.

So what should she do? Apologize again for interfering? Give Reed time to set aside possible anger and decide they belonged together despite everything?

The idea of waiting was unacceptable. Ludicrous. She wasn't going to stand by wasting time. Not when she could act. If facing her enemies had taught her anything, it was that life was short and should be lived to the fullest.

Overflowing with love for this man, Abigail leaned away slightly and gazed up at Reed while the traumatized boy celebrated by giving high fives to some of his fellow captives as they were unshackled.

Reed's cheeks were visibly streaked, as were hers, and she rejoiced. If he had not cared, deeply, he wouldn't be showing emotion so openly. Now was the time.

She started to say, "I…" and was silenced immediately by the most amazing kiss she'd ever experienced. Myriad thoughts swirled through her consciousness. She slipped both arms around his neck. Not only was Reed not angry, he seemed more than ready to hear what she intended to say.

As soon as he broke contact she tried again. "Reed, I…"

Another kiss. Another thought ended in the beauty and assurance of his affection. Dare she try again? Was it even necessary?

With her eyes closed and her heart wide open, Abigail let her thoughts thank her heavenly Father for leading her to this man and keeping them together long enough to fall in love. Then she tried to concentrate on how to tell Reed.

That would be easier to figure out if he wasn't kissing me senseless, she thought. This time, when he let her come up for air, she merely smiled.

That was apparently enough, because he mirrored her joy. "I hope you were trying to say you love me, because I'm head over heels in love with you, Ms. Jones."

"I was." The smile spread. Relief triggered humor. "Does this mean I get to keep training the puppy?"

"Only if I come along with her. We're a package deal."

"You are, huh? Are you well trained, Officer Branson?"

"Perfectly. I have the commendations to prove it." He was grinning broadly, his dark eyes sparkling. "I don't mean to rush you, I mean, you can take all the time you need. I'd just like your promise you'll marry me someday."

"Someday? Then we have a problem. Midnight needs specialized training ASAP whether she goes on to become a working K-9 for the police or serves some other purpose. I'm afraid we'll have to sacrifice for the sake of the dog and get married pretty soon."

His hearty laugh made her spirits soar. "I guess we will," he said. Then he kissed her. Again and again.

In the background, Abigail saw Dominic slowly walking away from them and her heart leaped. Was it feasible to become his guardian or even adopt him? she wondered. Was that asking too much?

Still in Reed's arms, she raised on tiptoe to whisper the question in his ear. His answer wasn't immediate, but he did seem willing to consider a family of three. That was good enough for Abigail. A husband, a son, a K-9 tracker and the perfect cuddly puppy. It was more than she had ever wished for. What more could she ever want?

EPILOGUE

It was Reed's idea to treat Abigail—and Dominic—to lunch at Griffin's. He wanted to show her the special areas designated for K-9 officers and their dogs as well as discuss their shared future in a homey, relaxing atmosphere. They had both decided it was time to tell the boy what they hoped to do and see if he was on board with adoption.

"You're sure we can take the dogs inside?" Abigail asked.

Reed smiled. "Sure can. The owner, Lou Griffin, designated a special section for K-9 officers and their dogs. He even added a sign that says The Dog House."

"Wow. Awesome."

Chuckling, Reed glanced at Dom, who had walked on ahead. "You're starting to sound like somebody else I know."

"Well, we have spent a lot of time together

lately." She sobered. "I wish I knew why he sometimes seems so unhappy."

"I think what we have to ask him will fix most of that," Reed said. He'd passed the wide front window and was reaching for the handle of the door before he noticed the hand-lettered note taped to the inside. It read, "Closed due to family emergency."

Cupping his hands around his eyes to cut the glare, he tried to see inside. The place looked deserted. Reed sighed in frustration. "Not good. I thought they were going strong when they re-opened after the explosion."

"Explosion?"

"Don't worry. It won't happen again. Like our kidnappers, the bomber is done causing trouble, although there are still developers who would love to get hold of this chunk of land and build something new here."

"I love the old neighborhoods and shops. It gives New York character."

"I know." Reed thought he saw something move inside so he decided to knock. "Hey, Lou! What's up? We're starving here."

A grumpy-looking gray-haired old man with his arm in a cast opened the door and peered out. "We're closed. Barb has the flu and as you can see, I won't be able to get orders up fast enough by myself. Sorry."

"Aw, c'mon, Lou. At least a cup of coffee. There's no other place around here that allows dogs."

The door swung back. "Okay, okay. Coffee. I'm always open for my buddies in uniform and their K-9s. I've got some Danish left. Or pie." He eyed the wiry, dark-haired teen with them and arched a bushy brow. "Who's your friend?"

Reed placed a proprietary hand on Dominic's thin shoulder and looked to Abigail for unspoken permission. When she nodded, he said, "I'd like you to meet Ms. Abigail Jones, who has agreed to marry me. And this is Dominic. He'll soon be our son if he agrees to being adopted."

The old man gaped, then recovered and stuck out his good hand to shake Reed's. "Well, I'll be. When you do it, son, you go all the way. Instant family. Congratulations."

Abigail lightly patted the boy's opposite shoulder. "What about it, honey? We talked about this a few days ago and you seemed open to the idea so we've looked into it. What would you say to having a couple of new parents?"

"You guys were serious? Yes!" His shout startled both Jessie and Midnight into a chorus of barking while the adults laughed.

"Let's go sit in there," Reed said, gesturing at the French doors leading to the separate section Lou kept for officers and their dogs.

By the time they'd settled down around a table, they were joined by Reed's commander, Noah Jameson.

Reed stood to shake his hand, then made introductions, inviting Noah to join them.

"I can't stay. I just stopped because I saw you come in," Noah said. He pulled out his cell phone as he glanced at Dominic. "Is this the teenager who had Snapper?"

Defensive, Reed was quick to say, "Only for a little while."

"Fine," Noah said, displaying the composite Dominic had done with Danielle and holding it out for him to look at. "Is this pretty close to the way you remember the man?"

Dominic nodded.

With a telling sigh, the interim chief put the phone back in his pocket. "I'd like to believe that's the face of my brother's killer." He focused on Reed. "What do you think?"

Although he trusted his son-to-be, Reed realized it had been a long time since Snapper had been handed over. Memories were funny things, as he and Abigail well knew. Still, he wanted to be encouraging as well as support the teen.

"I think that's the best, most logical assumption to make," Reed said. "We'll get the guy. None of us will give up or rest until he's behind bars."

The strong emotions he read in Noah's expression hinted at a desire for revenge. If Reed hadn't known what dedicated cops the remaining Jameson brothers were, he might have worried about a vendetta. He wouldn't have blamed them.

Gazing at his loved ones, Reed silently thanked God that they had made it through their personal crises. Abigail was going to be his wife, Dominic was eager to become their son and even Kiera had mellowed enough to return to the foster parents who had been so worried about her welfare.

Now it was time for him and his unit to go back to rallying around the Jameson family and work on solving their mystery. Justice was waiting.

* * * * *

If you enjoyed Trail of Danger,
look for Lani and Noah's story
Courage Under Fire *and the rest of the*
True Blue K-9 Unit *series from*
Love Inspired Suspense.

True Blue K-9 Unit:
These police officers fight for justice with the
help of their brave canine partners

Dear Reader,

Here we are again with wonderful K-9s and their capable partners in uniform. Because this series is a work of fiction, we have taken a few liberties with procedure and rules in order to make the complicated plots work. For instance, it is highly unlikely you would find siblings assigned to the same unit. In the case of this book about human trafficking, there would also be a more gritty background. Life on the streets is harder than any of us with warm homes and plenty of food can imagine.

On a lighter note, I ran away from home once. I packed snacks, hopped on my bicycle and pedaled off. Know what happened? I got to the street corner, remembered I was forbidden to cross by myself, and pedaled around the block until my snacks were eaten and I got hungry! My parents never even missed me.

I ran from my heavenly Father too, but he brought me back to Him. Remember, it's never too late to turn around and pedal home. The door will be open.

I can be reached by email at Val@Valerie-Hansen.com.

Blessings,
Val

THE FORTUNES OF TEXAS COLLECTION!

18 FREE BOOKS in all!

Treat yourself to the rich legacy of the Fortune and Mendoza clans in this remarkable 50-book collection. This collection is packed with cowboys, tycoons and Texas-sized romances!